STANLEY FISHER:
Shark Attack Hero
of a Bygone Age

How Brave Men Faced

a Relentless Killer Shark

in a Small New Jersey Town

the Summer of

1916

John Allan Savolaine

Book Design by Suzanne Anan

Published by Riverside Prints

ISBN: 9781630750343

First Edition

"To my wife, Cathy, my son, Clark, and my two grandsons,

Grant and Lee. They love history as much as I do."

December 25, 2018

To Thomas,
    I hope you enjoy
reading about our
Matawan hero, Stanley
Fisher.
    Best wishes,

John "CW" Bevolaqua

Acknowledgments

The author has collected data on this subject for several decades. Details with regard to names, locations, sequence of events, and relationships have come from local sources. Comments of contemporary residents and records of organizations have revealed valuable, practical information about Stanley Fisher. The now defunct *Matawan Journal*, which was published between 1869 and 1973, was an extremely valuable resource for detailed and colorful information. The archives of the Matawan Historical Society provided diaries of residents, voting records, and documents that filled in many gaps. The author's contacts with the Andersen family in Minnesota, direct descendants of Stanley Fisher, provided personal details not available in other sources. Also, special thanks to The Matawan-Aberdeen Public Library, especially Susan Pike, for town related material. Thank you to local residents who shared stories and anecdotes which were very helpful, especially Elizabeth Henderson, Howard Henderson, Jerry Hourihan, Jr., Glenn Pike, Patricia McKeen, F. Howard Lloyd, Helen Henderson, Thomas Henderson, and Walter Jones. Jennifer Skinner, a direct descendant of Captain Thomas Cottrell, shared helpful information about the Cottrell family. Carol Mandeville, granddaughter of Koert and Meta Wyckoff, also provided helpful family information. Thank you to Sally Arbegast and Sue Grove who read the manuscript and gave helpful comments. Historical photographs are from the archives of the Matawan Historical Society. Thanks to Robert Montfort, President of the Matawan Historical Society, for use of images in his personal collection. Other images are from the author's collection. And finally, special thanks to my wife, Cathy, for reviewing and editing the manuscript.

Introduction

This is a story about real people, specifically about a young man, Stanley Fisher, a twenty-four year old, handsome, popular, novice businessman just beginning his career as a tailor in the early Twentieth Century. It is also a story about life in a small town in a bygone age. The place is Matawan, New Jersey located in the middle, or Bayshore section, of the State. While not actually on the coast, it is only one and one-half miles from Raritan Bay and the Atlantic Ocean, and is considered the northern most tip of the Jersey Shore.

Stanley Fisher on July 12th, 1916 will lose his life and become a folklore hero in New Jersey as a result of a violent, public shark attack. Stanley was trying to recover the body of an eleven-year old boy, Lester Stillwell, who had fallen victim to a large shark at a muddy swimming hole along the banks of a tidal body of water known as Matawan Creek, which winds through the center of this small town like a snake. This incident, which was reported internationally at the time, is still remembered today, and was an inspiration for a multitude of documentaries, books, television shows, and movies.

This book is not a scientific study about the different types of killer sharks and their feeding habits. As a historian, I will tell a story. The focus will be on how a small New Jersey town and its local "favorite son" reacted to an unexpected, horrible tragedy on a typical hot summer day 100 years ago. It is an inspiring story of how everyday people took care of each other and dealt with a mortal crisis thrust upon them in the form of a relentless killer shark. Obviously, the world is now very different from the late Edwardian times and lifestyles of 1916 Matawan, but many human characteristics, fears, personality traits, and exceptional inner strength are still part of our makeup as human beings today.

In this book I will provide new, personal information concerning the background and character of this heroic young man, Stanley Fisher, who lost his life trying to recover the body of his young friend, Lester Stillwell, in the muddy shark infested waters of Matawan Creek on July 12, 1916. I invite the reader to get to know Stanley as a real-life person even though he lived in a different, distant time period. Walk the streets of 1916 Matawan and be ready for an adventure. You will see why his story has relevance today and how it has captured the interest of people around the world whenever the term "shark attack" is mentioned in the media.

Contents

Chapter | I

Matawan, 1916,
A Small Peaceful Town

To go back in time to try to understand the interaction of personalities and sequence of events of the 1916 tragedy, we must first take a good look at the setting of our story, Matawan, New Jersey. This small town had a population of about 1,500 people, in 1916. It is located about 11 miles from the open Atlantic Ocean coast, but only 1½ miles from Raritan Bay which indents into the eastern side of the state. However, Matawan is connected to the ocean by a tidal river known as Matawan Creek. It was only 30 feet across at the wider points, but was over 18 feet deep at high tide, at the time.

In the 18th Century ocean going sloops and schooners came in through the creek to the town known as Middletown Point in those days. During the Revolutionary War corn was shipped from this area to support George Washington's Continental Army. In the 19th Century 200 foot steamboats came into the creek along the wharves to pick up cargos of bricks, agricultural goods, porcelain tiles, utensils, and other items to take to New York and points north and south to Charleston and Savannah. When the railroad came to Matawan in 1875, Matawan Creek, or the "crick" as locals called it, was used less for commercial purposes.

Matawan, with its large stately Victorian mansions on Main Street was not a typical "shore town." Just a few blocks away from the central area there were numerous farms, orchards, and gardens. There were also several small factories in the area. Many sea captains had retired in Matawan, so that to hear someone addressed as "Captain" on the street was quite common. Most locals thought of Matawan as being "connected" to the sea but not actually a coastal town.

Being a very small town, Matawan did not have a sophisticated system to provide for public services. It did not have a traditional police department. The town Marshall, John Mulsoff, was also a local barber. The assistant Marshall, Bart Tice, was a baker. The chief of the volunteer fire department, Levi Emmons, Jr., was a blacksmith. When there was an emergency the residents had to really pull together to handle the crisis. In 1901, there had been a major fire that destroyed 11 businesses, the town opera house, and many private residences. Fortunately, along with many fearless volunteer fireman, a change in the direction of the wind saved the rest of the town from being consumed by flames.

A local weekly newspaper, the *Matawan Journal*, was read by virtually everyone in town. In addition to national, state, and local news, the *Journal* revealed interesting personal information and stories about residents including weddings and funerals in great detail, graduations, criminal activity, baseball scores, lodge news, and especially tidbits about society parties, and what was on the menus of church and firehouse social events. It was important to the residents to know what was going on and who was doing what in this small town.

The people in Matawan in 1916 were well aware of the fact that the World War was raging in Europe and in other parts of the world. The United States still maintained its neutrality, even after the sinking of the Lusitania in 1915, with the loss of over 100 American lives on board. Even with official neutrality, the United States was the major supplier of war material to the Allied side in the war.

However, Matawan was involved in world affairs in another way. Pancho Villa, the Mexican revolutionary, was causing trouble with raids across our southern border. In fact, the sitting mayor of Matawan, William H. Sutphin, who was also a sergeant in a cavalry troop in the New Jersey National Guard, was serving on military duty on our southern border with General John J. Pershing, Commander of the American Force sent by President Woodrow Wilson to counter the threat from Pancho Villa. Arris Henderson, the head of the town council, was fulfilling the role of "acting mayor" of Matawan in the summer of 1916 while Mayor (Sergeant) Sutphin was on military duty.

It is now time for our leading character, Stanley Fisher, to enter this tranquil scene in the summer of 1916. The Fisher family had been very prominent in Matawan for many years. They lived in a large two-story house on Fountain Avenue near the center of town. Captain Watson H. Fisher, Stanley's father, was born in Massachusetts, but came to live in Matawan with his wife Celia in 1879. Watson Fisher went to sea as a boy and worked his way up the profession to the rank of captain. He was now the "Commodore", or senior captain, of the Savannah Steam Ship Line. Through the years the Fisher family was also growing. Two daughters, Agusta and Florence were born in 1879 and 1888. Their only son, Stanley, was born April 12th, 1892.

In 1916, at age 24, Stanley was a tall, handsome, engaging young man who was easily noticed in a group. He was very popular in town to people of all ages. The young boys followed him around because they admired his strong build and athletic ability. Stanley was also an accomplished singer in the local Methodist Church choir. He was an officer in the YMCA organization and also enjoyed working with the town boy scout troop. He was always willing to give advice or a helping hand to young people who looked up to him as a role model.

Stanley Fisher, in the summer of 1916, was just starting a new business of dry cleaning and tailoring. Dry cleaning, while it technically goes back to the ancient Romans who realized that chemicals other than water did a better job of cleaning their togas, became a viable industry in the early part of the 20th century with the development of a successful non-gasoline based solvent.

Stanley's business was located in a building almost in the center of town. Stanley had also become the authorized resident dealer of the Royal Tailors, a men's clothing company home based in New York City and Chicago. Stanley had placed several impressive advertisements in the *Matawan Journal*, emphasizing how this new process would keep men's clothing in much better condition. He was proud to be a part of this new, developing technology.

Although Stanley was part of one of the most prominent families in town, he was not viewed as an upper class person of privilege. In Matawan, wealthy families often lived next to families of more moderate means. Interaction between the different economic classes was a daily activity. Communication among these groups was usually very cordial. They went to the same churches, belonged to the same lodges, and served the community together as members of the same volunteer fire companies. Most residents actually knew each other and felt comfortable saying hello as they passed on the street. In the event of a funeral, most people in town would either attend or send their sincere condolences. Matawan was really a nice place to live.

Another character in our story that we must introduce is "Matawan Creek" itself, or the "Crick" as it was known to residents. By 1916 the crick was not used as much for commercial purposes since the railroad had come to town, but it did have a sentimental attachment to those who had been born and raised in Matawan. To illustrate this, a poem appeared in the *Matawan Journal* on May 23, 1912 with the title, "The Crick", written by a local resident, Frank Doolittle, who had lived along the banks of Matawan Creek in his boyhood in the 1870s:

"The Crick"   by Frank Doolittle

Some call it "crick" and others creek
As does the dictionary

To "crick" I'll stick till River Styx
No more is crossed by ferry

A snake laid out its winding course
According to tradition

That's handed down to present day
By folks of erudition

It always fascinated me
Since I first can remember

I loved it when the year began
And ended in December

When I was but a little lad
I'll mention by digression

That I was still in pinafores

It made its first impression

It lured me to VanNesse's dock

Together with my brother

Though after warned to keep away

By a most careful Mother

Within the crick I learned to swim

But quite involuntary

A big boy pushed me off the brink

His way of being merry

T' was sink or swim, and no mistake

Decision came that minute

No time to think "I cannot swim"

When overboard right in it

I splashed with hands and kicked with feet

And made a great commotion

And somehow safely reached the bank

But swallowed half the ocean

I pity those who never bobbed

For eels or caught a shiner

And if the catfish should bite good

What sport could there be finer

Old "crick" my playground and friend

How much indeed I owe you

Permit me in my feeble way

My deference to show you

Today the "crick" is near filled up

And gone its ancient glory

And someday will come to an end

As does just now my story

This poem became very popular and was recited in school and around the town. It shows that this winding tidal creek had almost a mystical attraction to the people of this small Bayshore town.

However, a dark frightening shadow was moving toward this idyllic, peaceful little town. On a hot, humid, summer afternoon, July 12, 1916, this age of innocence was about to end abruptly in the splashing muddy waters of Matawan Creek. But before this happens, we will take a closer look at the early life of our future hero, Stanley Fisher.

Chapter II

Stanley's Boyhood Years

Captain and Mrs. Fisher had been living in Matawan since 1879. They had built a stately two-story house on Fountain Avenue, a tree lined area near the center of town. Their oldest daughter, Agusta, had a healthy, happy childhood and would grow to adulthood. Their second daughter, Florence, was not as fortunate. She died of pneumonia at home in July of 1889, at the age of 9 months, 21 days. Florence had been a happy, good natured child and the family was broken hearted when they looked at the empty crib and cradle.

The Fishers were thrilled when their third child and only son, Stanley, was born on April 12, 1892. Captain Fisher was granted a two week leave of absence to be with his family in the summer. Having recently lost a child, the Fishers would have been very concerned about Stanley's physical health. Fortunately, Stanley seems to have been a robust baby with no serious childhood illnesses.

As captain of a ship, Watson Fisher had a very demanding schedule steaming between New York and Savannah, Georgia. The *Matawan Journal* reported that he was able to have his Christmas dinner at home in Matawan for 1892. This was truly a joyful day for the happy young family. Mrs. Waters, Stanley's grandmother on his mother's side, was also living with the Fishers on Fountain Avenue to help tend to Stanley's early needs.

At the appropriate age, Stanley was enrolled in the primary school of the Glenwood Institute, a prestigious private school in Matawan, a few blocks away from the Fisher home. Most prominent families in Matawan regarded the Glenwood Institute as the right place to begin a good, thorough education as a foundation for a successful life. Garrett Hobart, the vice-president of the United States under William McKinley, had attended the Glenwood Institute. Robert Laird Borden, the Prime Minister of Canada during World War I, had taught mathematics and philosophy at Glenwood early in his adulthood.

Stanley was well-liked by the other children at the Institute. The teachers were pleased with his enthusiasm and progress in his studies. He wanted to be a leader whenever he had the chance in the different activities. Stanley also developed skill as a singer and was called upon to perform at school functions. He was very self-confident and enjoyed declamation activities and reciting poetry.

As a schoolboy Stanley was becoming recognized around town as a talented young fellow who really enjoyed performing. The Fisher family was proud of their boy and encouraged him during these formative years. In June of 1900 at the Glenwood Institute commencement of their "little folk" primary department, Stanley had an opportunity to really perform before a live audience. He sang a vocal solo which received prolonged applause by appreciative parents according to the *Matawan Journal*. He also recited two poems: "Three Bells" and "Nora, I Adore Her". In the awards section of the program, he received a silver medal for best recitation.

As Stanley was getting older, Captain Fisher took him and other members of the family on many voyages from New York to Savannah. In May of 1903 Captain Fisher assumed the command of the new steamship The City of Macon, of the Savannah Steamship Line. In its maiden voyage, Captain Fisher took the entire family, including Stanley's grandmother, Mrs. Waters.

During these voyages, Stanley was beginning to see his father in the role of "commander" of a ship with the lives of everyone on board in his capable hands. He could see the deference the crew and the passengers displayed to this leader. Captain Fisher had a sterling reputation. He had never lost a vessel or a single human life. He had performed heroically when he once rescued and towed a burning ship to port saving many lives.

Stanley was very proud of his father and was beginning to recognize him as a role model. In the early part of the 20th century the Victorian concept of "manhood" was still a goal young men would strive to achieve. Part of this responsibility was to protect women, children, and others who might need help in a dangerous situation. Organizations like the YMCA and the Boy Scouts of America also fostered these ideals.

Stanley had many friends in the neighborhood and enjoyed playing ball with them and romping around the woods nearby. A special friend was a neighbor, William "Willie" Shephard, who was the son of town councilman George Shephard. Stanley was a few years older than Willie, but they enjoyed each other's company. However, in July of 1903, their fooling around would cause a scare to both boys. Willie was perched on top of Stanley's shoulders and as they romped around, Willie fell backward off Stanley's back and hit the top of his head and was rendered unconscious for some time. Fortunately, Willie recovered with no permanent injuries. Both boys would remember this incident and laugh about it for years. As you will see, their young lives are going to be connected again 13 years later in July of 1916 on the banks of Matawan Creek.

As Stanley grew into adolescence, it became clear that his strong physical stature would be an advantage in athletics. He became a powerful swimmer and excelled at field sports. He enjoyed assuming the role of leader when he played in games. Stanley was never a "snob" and the other boys liked and respected him for his friendly, outgoing nature.

It is interesting to note that Stanley's full name was Watson Stanley Fisher. Named after his father, Captain Watson Fisher, Stanley used "W. Stanley Fisher" when he wrote his full name. Most of the time he was referred to as just Stanley Fisher when he was mentioned in articles in the *Matawan Journal* during these years. It is not clear whether Stanley, or his parents, originally preferred the use of "W. Stanley Fisher." Either way, it seems there was a desire to give Stanley some degree of separation from the moniker of his highly respected father.

Stanley's older sister, Agusta, was also very popular among young people in town. The other girls called her "Gussie" Fisher and she was invited to many parties and social gatherings. Stanley was very close to his older sister and they got along famously. Things were looking good for the Fisher family. Commodore Fisher had a very secure position with the Savannah Steamship Company and everyone in the family was healthy at a time when serious epidemics could come to town and totally devastate a family.

In October of 1907, Agusta Fisher married Arthur Nichols, a very talented and ambitious young man. The wedding took place at the Methodist Church on Main Street and the reception was held at the Fisher home on Fountain Avenue. There were many guests at the wedding and reception. Stanley's friends also attended the festivities. One of his special friends, Koert Wyckoff, was there. Koert would play an important role in what would happen later in July of 1916.

With Agusta's marriage to Arthur Nichols, Stanley would find another "role model" in his new brother-in-law. Arthur Nichols was a landscape architect. He had some creative ideas that would later bring him fame. Unfortunately for Stanley and his parents, the marriage would involve a move for Agusta and Arthur to Minneapolis, Minnesota where Arthur would pursue his new career.

Stanley would now attend the new Matawan High School on Broad Street where he could continue his involvement in public speaking and would have an opportunity to play in organized sports. He was becoming a handsome young man with an engaging personality to match. At this time, the future looked very promising for young "W. Stanley Fisher."

Chapter | **III**

Young Man About Town

While Stanley was attending high school, he was being noticed by people in town in various ways. He was developing a powerful physique and his love for strenuous exercise and sports made him a valued team member. He enjoyed getting out and riding his bicycle all around the Bayshore area. On his excursions, he met new people and made friends easily. The *Matawan Journal* reported that he had flat tires on occasion and had to walk his bicycle home. However, this never discouraged Stanley.

Stanley was certainly also being noticed by the girls for his striking good looks and his sparkling personality. When the guests to a party were described in the *Matawan Journal,* Stanley is frequently mentioned enjoying the ice cream and the parlor games. In the summer there were picnics and youth gatherings at the many farms around Matawan. In the winter the young people in town enjoyed ice skating and sled riding down Carriage Factory hill, also known as Ravine Drive.

Stanley continued to go on voyages with his sea captain father, Commodore Watson Fisher. As Stanley matured he related more to the "manly" qualities and commanding presence of his father on board ship. Captain Fisher was a careful, thoughtful leader who was always concerned about the welfare of those in his care. His word was law at sea, but he exercised this power with kindness and consideration. Stanley loved and admired his father, and he appreciated the fact that Captain Fisher gave him room to explore and develop his own ideas about what to do in life.

Stanley also had another successful role model during these formative years, his brother-in-law, Arthur Nichols who was eleven years older than Stanley. Originally from Massachusetts, Arthur attended the Massachusetts Institute of Technology and was the first graduate in their new landscape architecture program in 1902. In Minnesota Arthur was recognized in high places for his skill as a landscape architect. Arthur was chosen as one of nine men to serve on the Council of the Lincoln Highway, a direct highway from the Atlantic to the Pacific coast. He also designed a model city near Duluth, Minnesota. Agusta and Arthur Nichols also had a young son in their family. Stanley often visited his sister and brother-in-law during the summers. The Fishers remained a very close knit family, even though separated by hundreds of miles.

During this time, Stanley's musical ability developed in an impressive way. He was a member of the Methodist Church choir and was performing as a soloist both in church and at other town events. His voice was gaining in strength and flexibility. Another member of the Methodist Church, Meta Thompson, started to see Stanley in a more romantic way. She and Stanley were seen talking and walking around town together. They were also noticed attending the same parties, as described in the Matawan *Journal*. Stanley was a good friend of Meta's relative, Forman Thompson. Stanley was also a member of the singing group, called the "Quintet" with Forman Thompson, and other friends George Harris, Koert Wyckoff, and Alfred Davis. The Quintet was asked to perform at a number of social events in the area. Two of their favorite songs were "Onward Christian Soldiers", and "America". Both of these musical pieces allowed for powerful and emotional vocal interpretation. Audiences often gave the Quintet prolonged applause after the performances.

Stanley also had a healthy sense of humor and could take chances in front of an audience. Stanley and his close friend, George Harris, performed in a dramatic play in the high school auditorium. The play had an unusual title," The Trial of Breach of Promise of Miss Stanley Fisher versus George M. Harris." The case was hilarious and the people of Matawan in the audience were divided on what the "verdict" should be. Stanley in his engaging way could perform on stage in woman's clothing without losing his self-respect. He was becoming a very confident and uninhibited young man, and the people in Matawan loved it.

When Stanley graduated from high school in 1909 he decided to attend the Freehold Military Academy located in Freehold, New Jersey, the county seat of Monmouth County about ten miles from Matawan. Stanley lived at home and commuted daily. In this way he continued his life in Matawan, which was more interesting now that he had become much closer to his girlfriend, Meta Thompson. Meta had plans to attend a commercial school in New York City.

While at the Freehold Military Academy, Stanley was elected as "Captain of the Boys Brigade." This gave him a chance to practice his growing leadership skills. Later in 1910, Meta Thompson graduated from her business course in New York City. Stanley and Meta had been dating and there were rumors that they might get engaged. However, for now, they seemed to need a little more time before a permanent relationship was announced.

In March of 1911, the Fisher family experienced a personal loss. Stanley's grandmother, Mrs. Louise Waters, passed away at the Fisher home. Stanley was very close to his grandmother and it was very difficult for him to say good-bye to his "Nana." She was buried at Rose Hill Cemetery next to Florence, Stanley's older sister who died as a child. As a young man, Stanley was learning how painful a death in the family could be.

As Stanley left the Freehold Military Academy in June of 1911 it was time to start thinking of a career path for the future. Would he follow in his father's footsteps and go to sea? Would he seek a career "on land" like his successful brother-in-law, Arthur Nichols? Fortunately, Stanley had a number of great personality traits that would help him in any career path. The people in Matawan felt confident that Stanley would make the right decision. He had so much going for him. Stanley was excited and ready to move forward. He knew that his family would always support his final decision, but what would it be?

Chapter | IV

Stanley Selects a Career

After considering his interests and a direction for the future, Stanley decided that a life at sea could be a rewarding experience, as his father had demonstrated, but it was not the career path that he wanted. In July of 1911 Stanley went to Minneapolis, Minnesota with his mother to spend the summer with his sister Agusta and her husband Arthur Nichols. In October, it was announced in the *Matawan Journal* that Stanley had accepted a position to learn the new dry cleaning business and would remain in Minneapolis for three months.

Stanley felt very comfortable living with his sister and her husband, because he was used to being part of a close knit family and he was in a large city starting a new career. Fortunately, Stanley had an out-going personality and blended in quickly with his new environment several hundred miles from his Jersey home.

Meta Thompson remained in Matawan. She became the organist in the Methodist Church. As time went on she started to date a choir member and good friend of Stanley, Koert Wyckoff. It seems that her romance with Stanley had waned, but in a friendly way.

Captain and Mrs. Fisher frequently visited the family in Minnesota. The *Matawan Journal* reported that Stanley planned to stay longer than the original three months and was now actively involved in the dry cleaning business in Minneapolis. He seemed to be happy in his new career in this growing business in the early 20th Century. Busy career men needed this type of service to look their best in this exciting world of expanding business and commerce.

In June of 1913, Captain Fisher retired from the Savannah Steamship Company after 41 years of dedicated service. This was a real "rags to riches" story for Watson Fisher, a young boy going to sea from Massachusetts. He had started as a cabin boy and had worked his way up to the supreme rank of Commodore of the steamship company, with the satisfaction of knowing that he had a flawless career, never having lost a life at sea. All of these accomplishments were fully acknowledged in his impressive retirement ceremony. Stanley was certainly proud of his legendary father, a true example of Victorian manhood and virtue.

In July of 1913, Watson Fisher inherited $10,000 from a relative who had passed away. In 1913, $10,000 was four to five times the median annual income. The Fisher family now had a sound financial standing at a time when the world was heading toward a possible conflict between the competing empires in Europe. Britain, France, Germany, Austria-Hungary and Russia were sitting on a powder keg and a sudden spark could lead to a world war. Captain and Mrs. Fisher did not have to worry about money. They could settle down to a comfortable and happy retirement and enjoy their children and grand-children.

In June of 1914, Meta Thompson and Koert Wyckoff got married in Matawan at the Methodist Church. The *Matawan Journal* described their wedding and reception in great detail. Their friends were very happy for this young couple, including their mutual friend, Stanley Fisher. Stanley missed his happy times and relationships in his hometown of Matawan, where everyone knew and cared about each other.

In February of 1915, it was announced in the *Matawan Journal* that Stanley was finally returning to Matawan after living for several years with his sister in Minnesota. Stanley's friends were thrilled with this new development. As Matawan moved into the spring season, Stanley was eager to bring his new dry cleaning experience to his home town. He had learned the basics in Minnesota. Now he could take the lead in establishing this service and gain recognition for contributing something new to this small, provincial town along the Bayshore. Stanley looked forward to moving back into his social circles and participating in his favorite town activities.

In March Stanley resumed his interest in the local YMCA program. At the annual meeting of this organization,

Stanley was elected secretary of the board of the Matawan YMCA. His friends, Adam Banke, George Harris, and Theon Bedle, were selected as trustees. Stanley was also appointed chairman of the committee for physical activities. Stanley already had a reputation for his superior athletic ability, and was admired by the young people in town. Stanley was also working with the Boy Scouts. He helped them in sports and directed them in musical activities. Stanley had great rapport with small boys and helped them feel confident to participate in group activities. Stanley relished this responsibility. On Sundays, he was a leader in the Sunday School at the Methodist Church. Stanley was certainly happy to be back in Matawan and involved in local activities.

In April of 1915, Stanley put an advertisement in the *Matawan Journal* letting the town know that he was opening a cleaning and pressing business on Main Street, Matawan. The service included steaming, pressing, and repairing clothes. He stressed the quality of his services:

Your personality is your greatest asset. My business is to keep you looking "Spic and Span". I help you enrich your personal appearance by cleaning, pressing, and repairing your apparel so thoroughly that you may be regarded as "Fine Appearing".

TRY ME - TEST ME - CALL ME

W. Stanley Fisher, 122 Main Street, Matawan, New Jersey

Stanley was certainly assertive and self-confident in his advertising. His friends were also helping to spread the word that Stanley Fisher is back!

In July of 1915, there was a special musical entertainment event at the high school auditorium to raise money for the public library. Everyone in town was planning to attend. Stanley Fisher was one of the featured performers at this fundraiser. He really hit the high point and was in rare form that evening. The applause for him was abundant and prolonged according to the *Matawan Journal*. The town was really celebrating the fact that one of her "favorite sons", Stanley Fisher, was back in his home town where he really belonged.

Stanley's social life was also reviving nicely. In November of 1915, there was a social announcement that Miss Mabel Emmons was having a masquerade party at her house with seventeen of her friends. Stanley was one of the few male guests. The girls were delighted to have the handsome, popular Stanley Fisher back in their social scene. Stanley was certainly not a "wall flower" and enjoyed the attention of his many friends.

In May of 1916, Stanley moved his business to a more prominent location on Main Street, known as the Gehlhous Block. He was now the authorized retail dealer for the Royal Tailors clothing line of New York and Chicago. Stanley boasted in an advertisement in May of 1916: "We are doing a splendid business and the best of it is that old customers are coming in for new orders—a splendid recommendation."

As the spring season changed to hot, humid, Jersey summer weather, Stanley felt that his return to Matawan had worked out very well. He was ready to bolt into high gear in his young life. He had also been singing with his close friends, Koert Wyckoff, Forman Thompson, Alfred Davis, and George Harris in the "Quintet" around town. They had performed at the fifth annual banquet of the Men's Club of Matawan. The Quintet bellowed out two of their favorite songs, "Onward Christian Soldiers" and "America." The Men's Club enjoyed the show and cheered aloud along with their applause for these fine young men who represented the future of Matawan.

This expression of support was great for Stanley's morale. His choice of career "on land" in his new dry cleaning and tailoring business was going to succeed in his beloved hometown of Matawan.

Chapter **V**

The First Shark Attack

Wednesday, July 12, 1916, was a middle of the week summer work day. The weather was warm, sunny, and very humid. The men wore straw hats and were often seen in their suspenders and shirt sleeves, with a coat slung over their shoulders. The women wore wide brimmed hats and long sleeved blouses to protect their skin from the sun. Some of the more fashionable women carried parasols.

Main Street was noisy and dusty. It was not paved, and a trolley track for an electric street car ran down the center of the street. The trolley would ring a bell to alert pedestrians, automobiles and horse wagons to get out of the way. The confusion would also lead to some unpleasant comments, when tempers would flare, especially on a hot summer day. There were still hitching posts for the horses near the shops and stores. But now automobiles and motor trucks were also seen along the streets.

People on this July day were running their usual errands like going to the bank, getting a hair-cut, stopping at the bakery, and of course gossiping with friends and neighbors. The younger men were busy at work clerking at the stores, working at the tile companies, brickyards, and barrel and basket factories. A few blocks from the center of town other men were working in the fields of their farms. At the Matawan House Hotel maids were busy making the beds and sweeping the floors. Some of the men were unloading beer barrels for the hotel tavern.

If you had time to read the newspaper, you would see that the war was continuing to rage in Europe. The great Battle of the Somme had started on July 1 in France. The British army had suffered almost 60,000 casualties on the first day of the battle. This "modern war" was hard to comprehend in the small New Jersey town. President Wilson was still maintaining a policy of neutrality and was desperately trying to keep America out of the European war. The mayor of Matawan, William "Bill" Sutphin, was on military duty in the cavalry with the New Jersey National Guard chasing the Mexican revolutionary, Pancho Villa, along the southern border with General "Black Jack" Pershing. But in Matawan, it was a lazy, hazy summer day.

The local boys were at their part time summer jobs or doing their chores around the house or the farm. Some boys were shining shoes in front of the Matawan house Hotel. The traveling salesmen and the businessmen were the best customers. Farmers and wagon drivers were not concerned as much about dusty or muddy shoes.

Stanley Fisher was busy in his dry cleaning-tailor shop going over the suit orders he would have to fill for the Royal Tailors Clothing Company of New York and Chicago. His old friend and neighbor Willie Shephard was helping him. Stanley's new business was carrying on an active trade. It was important to keep the men of Matawan "looking good and in fashion with the times," as Stanley would keep reminding the public with his advertisements.

Lester Stillwell, an eleven-year old boy, was noticing the heat and considering the possibility of an afternoon swim in Matawan Creek. Since Matawan did not have a beach on the ocean, the creek, or "crick", to the locals, was the best place to cool off on a hot summer day. A favorite swimming hole was at the old abandoned Wyckoff Dock located on the banks of Matawan Creek at the base of Dock Street, a short distance off of Main Street. The Propeller Wyckoff was a steam cargo vessel that used to come into Matawan on a regular schedule to haul loads of bricks and manufactured goods to New York and points north. However, the trips had been discontinued after rail transportation became available in the late 19th Century. The Wyckoff dock had not been used for commercial purposes since 1903, but the boys could still jump and dive off the remnants of the old dock to swim and cool off. It was a secluded area, so the boys could hang their clothes on a bush and swim in the nude. The girls rarely went near the muddy waters of Matawan Creek.

Lester was the youngest of the three sons of William Stillwell, who worked at the Anderson Basket Factory on Atlantic Avenue. The Stillwell boys also worked part time at the basket factory during the summer, helping their father make peach baskets for the produce sellers. Lester also suffered from a form of epilepsy, which the locals referred to as "the shakes." His older friends, Johnson Cartan, Frank Clowes, Charles VanBrunt, and Anthony Bubblin kept an eye on young Lester to help him if he would have an episode of the shakes. Albert O'Hara, another young friend closer to Lester's age, also played with the group.

It was not unusual in a small town like Matawan for boys from different social and economic backgrounds to play together and be friends. Johnson Cartan, Frank Clowes, and Charles VanBrunt came from families with established businesses in town. Lester Stillwell, Albert O'Hara and Anthony Bubblin came from working class families. The boys just had fun together and did not care about these different class distinctions.

Like any town, Matawan had a few residents who would be viewed as "characters" with some noticeable eccentric traits. Captain Thomas Cottrell, a former sea captain, born in Matawan, was well liked and recognized as a good story teller about life at sea. He had been on many voyages around the world and he knew his trade. He was now living at Brown's Point in Keyport, the town next to Matawan, near the mouth of Matawan Creek as it enters Raritan Bay. He operated a small fishing tackle shop near his home. He enjoyed his daily walks between Keyport and Matawan along the winding route of Matawan Creek. However, on July 12th, he would see something that he would never forget.

On the hot July day, Joseph Dunn, a twelve-year old boy from New York City, and his fourteen-year old brother

Michael, were visiting their aunt in Cliffwood, New Jersey, another place near Matawan Creek, between Matawan and the ocean. They were planning to meet their friend Jerry Hourihan, a sixteen-year old boy from Matawan. The boys were thinking about going swimming in Matawan Creek near the New Jersey Clay Company brickyard wharf, between Matawan and Keyport. They would have to look out for the watchman who would chase them off the property. However, the chance for a swim on a hot summer day was worth it.

As the 12:00 noon whistle blew in the various factories and workplaces in town, the workers looked forward to their noon meal and a needed rest on a very hot summer afternoon. The residents walking around town were milling about and trying to make the best of an uncomfortable situation. Some of the ladies who were sitting on their porches on Main Street used their hand fans with a little more vigor. It would be a long day. Little boys were playing marbles in the dirt and little girls were tending to their dolls and having imaginary tea parties. It seemed that the young children went about their activities with less concern about the oppressive heat.

About 1:30 in the afternoon Captain Cottrell crossed the trolley bridge across Matawan Creek near Brown's Point. He was returning from a morning of fishing. As he looked over the railing he saw a sleek, eight-foot form passing under the bridge heading upstream toward Matawan. Having been at sea for most of his life, he recognized this form as the body of a shark moving at full speed toward the center of this small unsuspecting town.

Captain Cottrell immediately recognized the danger of this situation and quickly made his way to the bridge keepers shack. He made a hurried telephone call to the Matawan Town Marshall, John Mulsoff, at his barber shop. His report of a shark moving up Matawan Creek toward the town was not taken seriously by the men in the barber shop. There had already been two shark attacks along the Jersey Shore at Beach Haven on July 1 and Spring Lake on July 6. Marshall Mulsoff knew that people were talking about sharks and thought they might be prone to imaginary sightings. In addition, Matawan Creek did not seem a likely location for an incident similar to what had happened on the Jersey Shore and the open Atlantic Ocean.

Captain Cottrell was furious with the casual response to his telephone call. He decided to proceed toward Matawan in his small motor boat to share this important warning with those who would take it seriously. He was convinced that lives would be at stake if anyone encountered the shark.

In the meantime, Lester Stillwell, after being excused from his part-time job at the Anderson Basket Factory was meeting with his friends Albert O'Hara, Johnson Cartan, Charles VanBrunt, Anthony Bubblin, and Frank Clowes. The boys decided to go for a swim at the old, abandoned Wyckoff dock on Matawan Creek behind the paper bag factory building. The boys could still dive from the old pilings along the dock. Since there were never any girls around the boys took off their clothes and went skinny dipping. It was more convenient this way without having to bring swim trunks and other paraphernalia that older people took when they went for a swim.

Unfortunately, Captain Cottrell had passed the Wyckoff dock in his motor boat heading toward town before the boys arrived for their fateful swim. They were completely unaware of any problem or danger lurking in the waters of Matawan Creek. This was just a typical hot summer day in their hometown and they were ready for some fun.

The boys were enjoying themselves by diving off the pilings and then swimming back to the dock. Lester was proud of the fact that he had learned to float on his back. As O'Hara, Cartan, and Clowes were swimming back to the dock, O'Hara was bumped by something rough. Albert then noticed that Lester was no longer behind them. The boys saw what appeared to be an old log moving in the water, which was the fin of the shark. The boys then heard Lester scream and saw him struggle in the reddish water. As Lester was dragged below the water line several times, they realized that Lester was gone. They panicked and scrambled onto the dock. In their state of shock, they fled from the area in the nude and ran up the hill on Water Street to Main Street, screaming that "A shark got Lester!" The boys then turned right onto Main Street, passed the railroad station and headed toward the center of Matawan. Local residents who encountered the boys did not know what to make of this crazy scene and the boys' wild comments about Lester and a shark.

Chapter **VI**

The Shark Attack Continues

Stanley Fisher reacted to the commotion on Main Street and ran to the front of his store, which was located near the corner of Little Street and Main Street. When Stanley heard the boys cry out about Lester, he knew that something was seriously wrong, but he wasn't sure about the shark reference. Stanley was afraid that Lester may have had a spell of the shakes. This could be a serious problem if Lester were in the water when it happened.

Stanley took a leadership role in this massive confusion and recruited two of his friends, George "Red" Burlew, and Arthur Smith to accompany him down to the Wyckoff dock to find out what was going on. George Burlew was about Stanley's age and had known Stanley in town for years. George was now a chauffeur, or driver, of one of the new automobiles, for a wealthy resident in town. Arthur Smith was in his early fifties. He was a carpenter in town and was well known by the residents who had hired him for many local jobs. He lived on Dock Street, very close to the Wyckoff area. A number of other concerned residents were also heading in that direction.

About the same time that this was happening at the Wyckoff dock, Joseph Dunn, Michael Dunn and Jerry Hourihan were starting to swim at the New Jersey Clay Company brick yard wharf, about half a mile downstream toward Keyport. They were unaware of the situation going on in Matawan. The boys enjoyed this particular location because it was deep enough to safely dive into Matawan Creek. Their only problem was to keep an eye out for the watchman who might interrupt their swim and chase them off the property.

Back at the Wyckoff dock it was quite clear that Lester had been attacked in the water and it was evident that Lester had drowned or been savagely mangled by the shark. It was now important to retrieve Lester's body, before the shark could drag any remains out to Raritan Bay. Over one hundred people were now at the dock standing by, not really knowing what to do in this gruesome situation.

In the 19th century and early years of the 20th century, death was a common fact of life for every family. However, it was very important for the relatives to have the body of a loved one to care for and memorialize with a funeral ceremony, especially in the case of a horrible tragedy like this. Lester may be dead, but it would certainly help if the family could have his tattered remains to find some sort of closure for this early death of a child in this extremely unnatural situation. This was the least that could be done for this grieving family by their neighbors and friends in town.

As the situation was becoming more organized at the dock, Stanley and his two friends decided to go out in the creek in a row boat and probe for Lester's body with long poles. They had been warned by several bystanders not to go in the water for fear of another brutal attack. No one at the Wyckoff dock wanted to see another death.

Stanley, Red Burlew, and Arthur Smith tried this safe approach from the boat for about one hour. It was not producing any results. It became evident to them that the longer they waited, the more likely the shark could take the body away forever. The three men decided that they would not allow this to happen to young Lester Stillwell.

They changed into their swimming trunks and went back out in the boat into the middle of Matawan Creek. There were a few deep spots where Lester's body might be found. They began to dive down to the bottom of the creek, and feel around in the muddy water for Lester's mangled remains. The people along the dock were worried and watched with breathless anticipation each time one of the divers would come to the surface. This was very tiring work, along with the great danger involved in this heroic effort.

More spectators were gathering at the Wyckoff dock as the news was spreading around town. There were now close to three hundred people watching intently along the banks of the creek. Men, women and children were witnessing these brave men risking their lives with each dive to the bottom of Matawan Creek.

Stanley Fisher was by far the most popular member of this exceptional group. The people in town had been reading about the Fisher family, and Stanley in the *Matawan Journal* for years. Everyone felt a certain pride in connection to this friendly, outgoing young man. Older men thought of Stanley as a role model for their own sons.

It must have been apparent to Stanley as he saw the people on the banks of the creek watching him that they were relying on him to handle this major crisis. He did not want to let them down. He wanted to recover Lester's remains for the family so they could say farewell to their son and have a proper funeral.

The three men were getting very tired with the intense physical effort to reach the deep bottom of the creek. They could not see anything down below, but they tried to probe around the area in a systematic way to locate the body. They had been probing for nearly an hour, and it was now about 4:00 P.M.

While bobbing around in the water, waiting to catch his breath and try again, Arthur Smith felt a rough surface cross over his body. He noticed a churning motion in the water. Stanley had just gone down and was returning to the surface with something under his arm. He exclaimed that he had found Lester. After the shark had passed by Arthur Smith it swerved in the direction of Stanley. The shark then attacked Stanley with full force and grabbed his right leg between the knee and hip. With this impact,

Stanley released his grip on Lester's body. The shark tightened its vice-like grip on Stanley's leg and pulled him under the water twice. As Stanley came up again he cried out "Help me." Arthur S. VanBuskirk, a county detective, and W.H. Byrne, Jr., who were in a motor boat nearby, went to Stanley's assistance.

In the meantime, Stanley was trying to swim toward the dock with his free leg. Being a large man he fought the shark with his fists with great force. The men in the boat tried to hit the shark with their oars. As Stanley approached the side of the crick, the shark crunched down and stripped the flesh to the bone on his leg. The shark then disappeared. Stanley was pulled into the boat and a rope tourniquet was hastily applied to stem the profuse bleeding from the open wound. Red Burlew and Arthur Smith were not in a position to help him at this point. They were both exhausted and partially in a state of shock. The people on the dock were also terrified and screamed at what they had just witnessed.

As Stanley was being moved onto the dock he saw his wound for the first time and exclaimed, "Oh, my God!" The nearby spectators also cringed on seeing the open wound and all of the blood and torn flesh. A quick search was made for a doctor to come to the scene, at first with little success. Then, Dr. George Reynolds arrived at the dock to try to stabilize the wound as much as possible. A more substantial tourniquet was applied and an effort was made to calm Stanley down to control the trauma.

Dr. Reynolds decided to send Stanley to Monmouth Memorial Hospital in Long Branch, New Jersey by train since the railroad station was very close to the Wyckoff dock. The only other practical alternative would be to take Stanley to Saint Peter's Hospital in New Brunswick, New Jersey. This trip would have to be by automobile and the roads were bumpy and unpaved. Dr. Reynolds felt that Stanley's wounds were too severe for this method of transport. The railroad station was nearby, but up an embankment. William "Willie" Shephard, Stanley's old friend, helped to carry him on an improvised stretcher up to the train station. Willie also readily volunteered to ride with Stanley on the train to the hospital. Most of the people in town were waiting anxiously at the station for the next train to Long Branch, which would arrive at 5:06 P.M.

While all this activity was going on in Matawan, the three boys, Joseph and Michael Dunn and Jerry Hourihan were at the New Jersey Clay Company brickyard wharf enjoying an afternoon swim. They were completely unaware of what had happened at the Wyckoff dock earlier. Then, they heard a motorboat approaching from the direction of Matawan. Men were shouting to get out of the water because there had been a shark attack. Captain Thomas Cottrell and Jacob Lefferts, a Matawan lawyer, had arrived on the scene at the brickyard wharf.

The boys were informed that a shark had attacked Lester Stillwell and then Stanley Fisher. The three boys were now trying to get out of the water as quickly as possible. The two older boys, Michael Dunn and Jerry Hourihan, climbed out of the water first. The youngest boy, Joseph Dunn, was about to leave the water when the shark grabbed his leg and pulled him back toward the center of Matawan Creek. At this point, Michael and Jerry jumped back into the water to try to pull Joseph away from the shark. Jacob Lefferts, on seeing this, jumped into the water with his clothes on, to help the rescue effort. When the shark finally released its grip on Joseph's leg, the others were able to haul Joseph into Captain Cottrell's boat. The wound to Joseph's foot and lower leg had shredded the flesh, but fortunately had not severed the artery.

Captain Cottrell and Jacob Lefferts decided to take Joseph back to the Wyckoff dock area where some immediate medical attention might be available. When they arrived at the dock, Dr. Reynolds was still working with Stanley at the railroad station. However, Dr. Herbert Cooley, from Keyport, was now at the scene to provide medical attention. Dr. Cooley used his skills to perform emergency treatment. He determined that Joseph's wound, while not as substantial as Stanley's, was still very serious and prone to infection. Joseph was conscious and able to communicate. He said he was from New York City, but he was hesitant to give his street address. He did not want his mother to be worried about his injuries. Dr. Cooley decided to send Joseph to Saint Peter's Hospital in New Brunswick by automobile because the bleeding was under control. This method of transport seemed to be appropriate in his situation.

Stanley Fisher was at the Matawan Railroad station waiting for the 5:06 P.M. train to take him to the Monmouth Memorial hospital. He was weak but trying to tell his friend Willie Shephard what had happened in Matawan Creek. Willie had volunteered to accompany Stanley on the train ride to Long Branch. Several times Stanley confirmed that he had hold Lester's body at the time the shark attacked him. At the moment of impact Lester slipped away from his grasp. When the 5:06 train arrived, Stanley was carefully placed in the aisle between the seats, with Willie by his side. He was still conscious and thanked the people who were attending to him.

When the train arrived in Long Branch Stanley was admitted to the hospital at about 5:30 PM. He was extremely weak at this point. The loss of blood and shock were taking its toll. Before surgery could take place, he was able to mouth some final words to the attending surgeon prior to his death at 6:35 PM. He said that he had found Lester at the bottom of the creek and had taken him away from the shark, which was still close by. He told the surgeon, "I got Lester away from the shark. I did my duty."

Stanley's last thoughts in this world were about Lester and what he felt he had to do regardless of the danger. In his mind, he had "done his duty" as a man, an honorable man, demonstrating selfless compassion for another human being. This was very much a part of the late Victorian era of what a good person, especially a man, should do. Stanley had fulfilled this special mission in his short life.

When word got back to Matawan that Stanley had died, the residents were shocked at this horrible development. Two of their friends and neighbors had been taken from them in this most unnatural manner by an invading shark in the middle of their safe, comfortable home town on a typical summer day in July.

In fact, Stanley's parents, Captain and Mrs. Fisher, were not even in Matawan at the time. They were visiting their daughter, Mrs. Agusta Nichols and her family, in Minneapolis, Minnesota. The acting mayor of Matawan, Arris Henderson, sent them a telegram at 10:00 P.M.

informing them of Stanley's death, but not explaining how he had died. The Fishers could not imagine what had happened to their healthy, physically strong, young son. They immediately made arrangements to begin the return trip to Matawan the next day.

In the meantime, Lester's body had still not been found. Many residents were still down at the creek trying to find a way to recover Lester's body before it disappeared forever out into Raritan Bay. Men were erecting mesh nets to try to confine the body to the creek and were setting off dynamite explosions to raise the body from the bottom of the creek. Men were firing shotguns and rifles at imaginary targets in the water. The people were working themselves into an emotional frenzy. They were determined to get Lester's body for the Stillwell family. Stanley had died trying to do this, and the people of Matawan were angry and determined to succeed.

Panic was now in the air around the entire coastal region. The men down at Matawan Creek were still trying to kill the shark and recover Lester's body throughout the night. However, other than the noise and confusion, nothing was happening. These Matawan attacks were the third, fourth and fifth shark attacks in the month of July, following the ones in Beach Haven, and Spring Lake earlier in the month.

This was now was becoming a national story.

Chapter | **VII**

The Days Following

The Fishers left Minneapolis the next day, Thursday, but did not arrive at the train station in Matawan until Friday morning. Agusta Fisher Nichols was with them and was pregnant. This was a horrible experience for a woman "expecting", especially in 1916 when the pregnancy time was treated with extreme care to avoid any problems for mother or child. Then, the worst possible thing happened. While en route to Matawan the Fishers saw a Chicago newspaper describing, "The Matawan Shark Attack", while they were changing trains at the Chicago railroad station. Until that time, they had no idea of how Stanley met his death. The original telegram they received only mentioned that Stanley had died, without going into

59

details. By now the story had become national and even international news, appearing in the *London Times*.

The Fisher family could not comprehend what was going on. Captain Fisher, a sea captain, could not believe that a killer shark could make its way up the winding course of Matawan Creek, a mile and a half from Keyport harbor and Raritan Bay. Why would a shark so viciously attack three different people? This was too much for the grief stricken family to bear. They still could not believe that Stanley was gone and would never say "good-bye" to this loving close knit family. They found it impossible to control their emotions on this endless train ride home.

Back in Matawan, newspaper feature writers and marine scientists were coming to this small Bayshore town to find out what had happened. Most of the guests were staying at the Matawan House Hotel on Main Street. Townspeople were patrolling the creek with their rifles and shotguns ready to slay the ruthless invader who had terrorized their town. They were also "posing" for eager photographers who were covering the event. Lester's body had still not surfaced on the next day. The men working at the creek were still hopeful that Lester's remains could be recovered. However, hope was slipping with every beat of the clock.

Then at about 5:15 A.M. on the morning of Friday, July 14th, the body of Lester Stillwell was discovered by Harry VanClief, an engineer on the New Jersey Central Railroad, and William B. Clayton, Jr., while walking along Matawan Creek going to work at the Matawan train station. The body had risen to the surface about 250 feet up the creek from where Lester had first been attacked.

After permission for removal of the body was obtained from the county physician, Dr. Harry Nefie, the Arrowsmith Brothers Undertakers took charge of the remains, identified by the parents, and took it to their establishment on Main Street. Undertaker W.E. Arrowsmith examined the body and commented in the *Matawan Journal*, "the left abdomen and left shoulder had been eaten away and the right breast was torn open. The left ankle had also been chewed off and the flesh between the hip and thigh mangled. The intestines were also torn open. The face however, was not disfigured." The Stillwell family was devastated with this horrible situation, but at least they had Lester back from the shark.

The Fisher family arrived in Matawan on Friday morning, July 14th. They were met at the railroad station by Tillie Holmes, a woman in her eighties, who had been a family servant for many years. Their first task was to make funeral arrangements for their beloved Stanley. They would also use the services of the Arrowsmith Brothers Undertaking establishment on Main Street. The family decided that Stanley's funeral would take place the next day, Saturday, July 15th, late in the afternoon at the Arrowsmith Funeral Parlor. The Stillwell family also decided to have the funeral for Lester the next day, Saturday, at their home on 47 Church Street at 2 P.M. in the afternoon. The Arrowsmith Brothers were also in charge of the arrangements.

The next day was a very sad time for the people of the small town of Matawan. Lester's funeral was at his home just a few blocks from the center of town. The Reverend Leon Chamberlain of the Methodist Episcopal Church presided. The family was overcome with grief.

Mr. and Mrs. William Stillwell were comforting their other children Russell, Harry, Ammie, and Gennie. After the service, Lester's body was carried to the motor hearse by his young friends John Larkin, Anthony Bubblin, Albert O'Hara, Daniel Morgan, Charles VanBrunt, and Clarence Bean. Lester was laid to rest at the new Stillwell family plot at Rose Hill Cemetery about a mile away on the other side of town, on Ravine Drive. This was a small, picturesque Victorian style cemetery situated at the highest point in Matawan. Reverend Chamberlain said the final prayers and two members of the Methodist Church choir, Miss Lillian Bolte and Koert Wyckoff, sang "Surrender All" and "Safe in the Arms of Jesus." The last hymn was often sung at the death of a child. Koert Wyckoff, one of the soloists was also the very close friend of Stanley Fisher. The location of the grave was at a point near the base of the hill in the cemetery.

Stanley Fisher's funeral took place later Saturday afternoon at the Arrowsmith Brothers Funeral Parlor on Main Street. There was an open casket viewing at 4:00 P.M. At 5:00 P.M. the service was conducted by two ministers, the Reverend Leon Chamberlain, the current minister of the Methodist Church, and by the Reverend B.C. Lippincott, a former minister of the Methodist Church and a close friend of the Fisher family. One of those attending the funeral was Tillie Holmes, Stanley's former nursemaid when he was a baby, and a family servant for many years. There were many flowers around the casket. Young friends were present from the many different groups that Stanley had been associated with around town.

Stanley's body was then moved to the motor hearse to be

taken to the Fisher family plot at Rose Hill Cemetery. The pall bearers were Stanley's close friends, F. Howard Lloyd, Harry Walling, Theron Bedle, Koert Wyckoff, Adam Bank and Henry Clark. A long line of automobiles followed the hearse to Rose Hill Cemetery, where additional services were conducted by the two ministers.

Since both ministers knew Stanley very well, their remarks were of a personal and touching nature. The *Matawan Journal* covered the sentimental references to Stanley's exemplary life. The ministers emphasized Stanley's high character and his generous caring spirit which he freely displayed to those around him. Stanley had influenced many young people in his short life. There were many members of the Sunday School, church choir, YMCA, and high school alumnae who knew and admired Stanley during his years in Matawan. His grave was next to his sister, Florence, who died as an infant in 1889, before Stanley was born. It was also near the grave of his grandmother, Louise Waters, who died in 1913. Stanley had visited these graves many times through the years. By a strange coincidence Stanley's grave is located almost directly above Lester's grave, which is on a lower part of the hill.

There was also an unusual development for the Fisher family during this unsettled time when they returned to Matawan. On the day of the funeral, a young insurance agent, Ralph Gorsline, approached Captain and Mrs. Fisher as they were returning from the cemetery. He expressed his condolences and then said that Stanley had a life insurance policy on himself which amounted at the time to $7,500. The Fishers were astounded. They had no knowledge that Stanley had taken out this policy.

This situation seemed unbelievable because Stanley had been a healthy young man with no chronic ailments. Ralph Gorsline explained that Stanley had accepted the insurance policy from his friend Ralph as payment for a new suit Ralph had acquired from Stanley's business. The beneficiary of the policy was Mrs. Watson Fisher. Captain and Mrs. Fisher decided to use the money to honor the memory of their beloved son. They later arranged to purchase a stained glass window for the Methodist Church to be dedicated to Stanley. This would be a fitting memorial for their son, who had devoted so much of his time and musical talent for the congregation.

It was still difficult for Matawan to find a sense of closure for this traumatic experience that had shaken their comfortable small town existence. The killer shark was still at large and newspaper reporters and photographers were milling around town and exploiting this sensational story. The acting mayor of Matawan, Arris B. Henderson, had offered a $100 reward to the person or persons able to kill the Matawan man eating shark.

The size of the wound in Stanley's thigh was about fourteen inches wide, with about 10 pounds of flesh removed. A shark with this size jaw could be close to eight or nine feet long and weigh four hundred or five hundred pounds. Many angry residents and fishermen hoped to claim this reward and end the threat this man eater posed to the Bayshore area. Various methods were being used by the shark hunters to find and kill their prey.

Dr. John T. Nichols, the fish curator and expert from the American Museum of Natural History in New York City made a fact finding trip to Matawan to verify if a man eating shark had caused the two deaths and mauling of a third victim. The terrible wounds to Lester Stillwell and Stanley Fisher confirmed the fact that a shark was responsible. Until this time, sharks were not considered a danger this far up the Atlantic coast by marine scientists. Dr. Frederick Lucas, the director of the Museum of Natural History, had previously believed that sharks were not the likely culprits of the incidents along the Jersey shore in July of 1916. However now there could be little doubt. The marine scientists were not quite sure which type of shark was the man-eater.

The shark hunters were actively searching for the culprit that had ravaged this small town in such a savage way. In fact, on the morning of July 14th, the day Lester Stillwell's body was discovered near the train trestle, two men, Michael Schleisser and John Murphy, set out in a small boat from the Bayshore town of South Amboy. Michael Schleisser also happened to be a lion tamer for a circus. The two men dropped a dragnet from the back of their boat to catch some fish. Soon, they were in an area near the mouth of Matawan Creek. Near the stern of the boat they noticed something large in their net. When they saw the black tailfin, they realized that they had caught a shark. It was thrashing around in the water and actually pulling the boat backwards, lifting the bow of the boat out of the water. Schleisser realized that the shark was about as long as the boat. The men struck the shark on the head with a broken oar that was in the boat. The shark became more entangled in the net. The men signaled a larger boat that was nearby, which then helped them tow the shark back to South Amboy. When the sharks bottom side was cut open on the dock, it revealed some bones and lumps of flesh in the stomach and intestines. These were identified by some local physicians on the dock as human parts. Michael Schleisser, who was also a noted taxidermist, took the shark's remains back to his New York workshop.

Dr. Frederick Lucas and Dr. John Nichols of the American Museum of Natural History and Dr. Robert Murphy, a marine scientist from the Brooklyn Museum, visited Michael Schleisser and saw the shark that he had captured. They determined that it was a great white shark. However, the bones found inside the shark could not be directly linked to Lester Stillwell or Stanley Fisher. Since the shark was found near the mouth of Matawan Creek it certainly was a suspect in the tragedy.

On July 15 the hospital spokesman at Saint Peter's Hospital in New Brunswick, said that Joseph Dunn would survive his wounds if infection did not set in. At first, Joseph was very weak due to the loss of blood. The doctors felt that Joseph might keep his leg if his condition stabilized. Joseph's mother came to see him from New York. It would be necessary for Joseph to be hospitalized for enough time to ensure that there would not be a relapse in his condition.

Joseph's father, James Dunn, made a request in the *Matawan Journal* on August 31, 1916, that concerned friends should understand that Joseph's recovery would be a long process. Mr. Dunn said that he had received letters from all over the country from people concerned about Joseph's health. He thanked those who had shown such interest in Joseph's welfare. Joseph was making good progress and he promised to put notices in the various newspapers updating Joseph's progress. The young boy would remain at Saint Peter's Hospital until September 4, 1916. It was likely that Joseph would have some limitations on the use of his lower leg and foot. Joseph was the only survivor of the total of five victims who were attacked in Beach Haven, Spring Lake, and Matawan.

The July 1916 shark attacks had made national and international news. Even President Woodrow Wilson was trying to deal with this shark problem using the resources of the Federal Government.

Gradually the tension would lessen a bit, because there were no more shark attacks after July 12th. Captain Thomas Cottrell produced a dead shark which he claimed was the man eater of Matawan Creek. He would receive the $100 reward offered by the acting mayor of Matawan, Arris Henderson. This shark may not have been the actual culprit. The payment of the reward however seemed to offer some closure to this traumatic experience. Also the people of Matawan knew Captain Cottrell and appreciated his actions on the day of the shark attack. He was the one who first saw the shark coming under the trolley bridge, tried to warn the people of Matawan, and he helped to transport Joseph Dunn to get medical help. He certainly did his part.

The residents of Matawan still could not understand the strange twist in the fate of Stanley Fisher. Stanley had watched his beloved father go to sea many times. He had traveled frequently with Captain Fisher on his voyages to Savannah and had a taste of life at sea. He was also a strong swimmer who really enjoyed this pastime. However, after weighing his personal desires and preferences Stanley had decided not to go to sea as a career, rather he decided to stay "on land" as a businessman in this new activity of dry-cleaning. He was to be a tailor and a sales representative for fashionable male clothing. His outgoing personality was a great asset in interacting with his customers. He wanted to enjoy the stability and regular hours of a local business in his hometown.

Instead, on July 12th, 1916, he found himself in mortal combat with one of the truly fierce predators of the sea, a shark in an inland waterway, the "crick." This whole situation seemed unnatural and wrong to the people of Matawan. What could be said to Captain and Mrs. Fisher when you saw them on the street?

On August 12th, Stanley's sister Agusta, and her family returned to Minneapolis, Minnesota. Mrs. Fisher went with them for an extended stay. It was difficult being at the Fisher home realizing that Stanley would never return. The family had made arrangements for a stained glass window to be created in Stanley's memory for the Methodist Church. The project would take quite a while to complete. It would be a lasting memorial for their beloved Stanley.

Chapter

Hardships Continue

Time moved on. The newspaper reporters, photographers, and marine scientists left Matawan to deal with other matters. The *Matawan Journal* went back to covering the usual local stories of lodge ceremonies, weddings, engagements, funerals, vacation plans, and inspiring sermons in local churches. The children played their games and their parents went to work to provide for their families. As the residents passed Matawan Creek they thought of Lester Stillwell and Stanley Fisher and often said aloud, "What a shame!"

In the spring of 1917 the United States entered World War I on the side of the Allies, France, Britain, and Russia.

Germany had resumed unrestricted submarine warfare and the United States could no longer remain neutral. The declaration of war in April had an effect on all parts of the country, and especially on small towns where every person knew and cared for their neighbors. In order to meet the manpower needs for a major European war, a draft law was passed by Congress. Young men were required to register for this new method of conscription. There were many local men who were eager to show their patriotism and immediately registered for the draft. The *Matawan Journal* published the results of their physical examinations. Some were able to meet the standards for military service, but many others were rejected for various ailments. It was often difficult to face your neighbors when you were rejected in this way.

The Matawan, the town mayor, William H. Sutphin, had returned from his duty with the cavalry pursuing the illusive Mexican revolutionary, Pancho Villa. He was now offered a commission as a first lieutenant in the new army air corps. Soon, he would again leave Matawan in the service of his country.

Several people involved in the shark attack would also serve their country in uniform. Frank Clowes, who had been the oldest boy down at the Wyckoff Dock on July 12, 1916 joined the navy. He was now 20 years old and a mechanic in his father's garage in town. Willie Shephard, Stanley Fisher's close friend who made the final journey with Stanley to Monmouth Memorial Hospital in Long Branch, also joined the navy. John Hourihan, a relative of Jerry Hourihan, the boy who helped Joseph Dunn get away from the shark at the New Jersey Clay Company brickyard wharf, joined the army and would later die in

France of the Spanish influenza which ravaged Europe and the United States in 1918.

It was important in Matawan that everyone supported the war effort in some way. Almost all the women in town were members of the Red Cross. They provided different items for the troops that might make life a little more comfortable. The Woman's Club of Matawan, which had been founded in 1915, was very active in this effort. Young girls attended social activities for the recruits in camp who were still learning how to be "doughboys." Older women did their part and served as chaperones at these social events.

The men in town who were too old to serve in uniform, or men who could not serve for health reasons, were ready to help out in other ways. Some worked in war industries, like the Thomas Gillespie Artillery Shell Loading Plant in nearby Morgan, New Jersey. There were also a number of women who had these jobs. It was dangerous work considering the fact that high explosives were being prepared for shipment to Europe. Women were often used as "inspectors" because they were extra careful and did not smoke.

Other men served in Civilian Home Defense groups. These were local residents who guarded the railroads, public utilities, and other potential targets that might attract enemy sabotage. In 1917 Captain Watson Fisher volunteered to serve in the Matawan Home Defense League as a guard. He was now retired from the Savannah Steam Ship Line and this activity would help him take his mind off the recent loss of his dear son. He also knew that if Stanley were still alive, he would definitely find a way to serve his country in time of war. By standing guard duty on a cold night, he knew Stanley would be proud and watch over him.

To Captain Fisher and the people of Matawan, Stanley had represented certain values and characteristics of nobility of spirit that can never really die. At the time of this national crisis, it was reassuring to remember men like his son. After all, one of Stanley's favorite musical selections as a soloist was "America." He always sang this stirring traditional song with great feeling.

The members of the Methodist Episcopal Church in Matawan were still waiting for the memorial stained glass window for Stanley to be completed. It was going to be called the "Bethlehem window." It would be placed in the front of the church, above the main entry door, so that the setting sun would shine through it at the end of the day. It would hopefully raise the spirits of those who gazed at it during this most horrible war in human history. The United States was now part of the "Big Push," with the influx of new aggressive soldiers and bountiful military equipment and supplies. The weary Germans, after four years of bloody warfare were now losing their will to fight. This last major allied offensive might finally end the carnage.

In April of 1918 the Fisher window was finally completed and delivered to the Methodist Church on Main Street. The town was very excited about the dedication service for this wonderful memorial for Stanley Fisher. The *Matawan Journal* of April 18th, 1918 described the service in great detail. The Reverend Lippincott gave an emotional sermon about his dear friend Stanley Fisher: "The high purpose of Stanley Fisher's life, his noble effort, his devotion to God and to his home are virtues that will survive and we hang them as garlands over his window today, using as our text John 15:13 'Greater love hath no man than this, that a man lay down his life for a friend.' His strength is perfected in beauty while his memories to his family and to his friends are as sweet and abiding as the smiles of the angels."

As members of the congregation wept openly, they read the dedication at the bottom of the Bethlehem window scene "In loving memory of Watson Stanley Fisher, April 12, 1892-July 12, 1916, Greater love hath no man." Stanley's longtime friend, F. Howard Lloyd, accepted the window on behalf of the church.

In the July 11, 1918 issue of the *Matawan Journal*, Stanley's sister Agusta Fisher Nichols, wrote a poem expressing how the family had to live with the sudden passing of their beloved son and brother.

It was hard to part with him

The one we loved so dear

The heart no greater pain could feel

No sorrow more severe

What pain he bore we will never know

We did not see him die

We only know that he is gone

And never said good-bye

The Fisher family found it difficult to find closure or any lasting consolation from their grief. Mrs. Fisher spent more time with her daughter Agusta and her family in Minnesota. Captain Fisher tried to be strong for his family. He also tried to do his duty in Matawan.

In October of 1918 another local tragedy affected the people of Matawan and the surrounding area. On October 4th, 5th, and 6th a series of explosions rocked the Thomas Gillespie Artillery Shell Loading Plant in nearby Morgan, New Jersey. In the explosions about 100 people were vaporized and disappeared, with unrecognizable body parts. The explosions also had a severe impact on surrounding towns. Windows were blown out from the concussion and the ceilings in many houses and buildings collapsed with the shock effect. The military instituted martial law to control any looting in the area. Residents were afraid to go into their homes during the continuing explosions for fear of structural failure.

The Morgan explosion also caused a crack in the new Fisher window in the Methodist Church. Fortunately, the stained glass tribute to Stanley did not shatter. It remained in place. It seemed to the members of the congregation that Stanley was still facing unexpected unnatural disturbances from an outside force.

The Morgan tragedy was also intensified by the fact that the devastating Spanish influenza pandemic of 1918 was hitting the Matawan area at the same time. This epidemic would eventually take the lives of over 675,000 Americans and between 50 to 100 million lives worldwide. Sixty-five residents died in Matawan. The two doctors in town were overwhelmed and neighbors and friends helped each other survive this crisis. A temporary hospital was set up in Matawan at the Grange Building on Broad Street. Unfortunately, the Morgan explosion caused many to gather together in groups rather than stay at home. This helped to spread the dreaded virus.

It is sad to note that many American soldiers in Europe who were fortunate enough not to be wounded or killed in combat would die from the Spanish Influenza. Several Matawan soldiers met their end this very way. John Hourihan was one of them.

When the armistice was signed in Europe on November 11, 1918, ending active combat in World War I, the residents of Matawan hoped that better times were ahead. The boys overseas would be returning home. The town prepared to welcome them back, and attempted to put the tragedies of the recent past behind them.

While the world events were changing, the Fisher family, Stillwell family, and many friends visited Rose Hill Cemetery and placed flowers on the graves of Lester and Stanley. It was still an unsettled topic of discussion at the barber shop, saloons, and social gatherings at the churches and fire houses. Residents looked at the "crick" and wondered how could all of this have happened in their town?

Chapter

Heroes of the Shark Attack

Stanley has been portrayed as a hero in the shark attack novels, non-fiction books, movies, and documentaries about the 1916 Matawan Creek tragedy. What does this really mean in terms of a human response to a crisis situation? How did Stanley Fisher's character development through the years influence his bold, decisive actions on July 12, 1916?

How do such powerful inner forces in a person lead to acts of heroism, and even self-sacrifice in a crisis situation? In Victorian times, it was believed that exposure to strong role models and solid moral training would prepare a boy to behave like a man when he reached maturity. This was a belief that led to the founding of the Boy Scout movement in the early 20th Century. It was believed that boys with proper training from dedicated male leaders and outdoor experiences would grow to become strong, reliable men who could handle difficult or even dangerous situations.

What about the Biblical role of being a "good Samaritan", a person who could not "look the other way" when others are in danger or suffering? Did Stanley see himself as a good Samaritan to the Stillwell family in trying to recover the body of Lester from the shark before it could be taken away forever. After all, Stanley knew Lester well. They both lived in a small town, and often played ball together. The people of Matawan looked up to Stanley Fisher and they believed he would do the right thing, even if it involved great danger.

Traditional heroism has typically involved a life or death situation, risking his or her life to save or protect another weak or injured individual. Many heroes are extremely humble and do not view themselves as exceptional or heroic. Audie Murphy, the most decorated American soldier in World War II, tried to deal with this in his autobiography, *To Hell and Back*, about his experiences in World War II. As a young man at the beginning of the war he had a slight physique and was turned down by the Marine Corps because he was too small to be a combat infantry man. He was also too young. His mother finally agreed to sign a waiver so he could enlist in the Army, which agreed to accept him.

Through his many death defying combat encounters described in *To Hell and Back*, he said he did "what he had to do." He never had time to thoroughly evaluate the risk involved. This did not mean he was not afraid. He freely admitted to this. He just did what he felt he had to do to protect his fellow soldiers during the war. No one ever denied his recognition as a "hero." The Congressional Medal of Honor did not even convince him that he was really a hero. He now rests in Arlington National Cemetery with other brave and modest heroes.

Women have also been ready to fill the role of heroine. A hundred years ago in 1915, a brave woman gave her life so that others would live. Edith Cavell was a British nurse working in Belgium before World War I. When the Germans brutally invaded Belgium, she decided to stay and live under their occupation. While she was working there, she helped British soldiers, who were prisoners of war, escape to the Netherlands. The Germans arrested her, put her on trial, and then executed her by firing squad. Her last words were "Patriotism is not enough." Her heroic act inspired thousands of British citizens to go to war.

Stanley Fisher at an early age read about heroes when he studied history in school. He also realized that his father, Captain Watson H. Fisher, was a very special person. People in town greeted Captain Fisher with respect and often sought his opinion on various local matters. Captain Fisher had also demonstrated great heroism in his career by rescuing passengers from a burning ship at sea. Stanley had observed his father take charge and do his duty while at sea.

On July 12, 1916, when the nude boys ran uptown shouting, "a shark got Lester", Stanley was one of the few who immediately realized that something was terribly wrong. He quickly ran to the dock and took charge, started the recovery operation and did what had to be done. At the Wyckoff dock close to three hundred people were watching him and the other two men, Red Burlew and Arthur Smith, risk their lives in shark infested waters. He was determined to locate Lester's body for his family. Stanley was one of the strongest men in Matawan at 6 feet one-inch-tall and 210 pounds. If anyone could succeed, it was Stanley Fisher. He was prepared to do his duty as a man.

Being a hero involves an action that is life threatening, where even self-sacrifice may happen. Stanley Fisher, George Burlew, and Arthur Smith were warned by many people at the Wyckoff dock not to go in the water. It was clearly evident at the time that Lester Stillwell had met a violent bloody death. Their attempts to dive down to recover Lester's body happened shortly after the original attack. The shark could still be in the immediate area. Each man knew that every dive down to the bottom of the muddy creek could be their last moment on earth. Why did they do it? They were not reckless, suicidal men. They all had loving families. There must have been another emotion in them that was just as strong as self-survival.

This feeling of immediate danger also applied to Michael Dunn and Jerry Hourihan when they jumped into the water to save Joseph Dunn at the New Jersey Clay Company brickyard wharf. Jacob Lefferts, the Matawan lawyer, also entered the shark infested waters to help Joseph Dunn. They knew that the shark was still there. It was pulling Joseph in the opposite direction. All of the people that day in the water were facing the possibility of a horrible agonizing death. However, they were able to function in spite of this obvious danger. As history would reveal, Stanley became a hero that day along with the others who had risked their lives in the muddy waters of Matawan Creek.

Other characters in this story behaved in a heroic way. Captain Thomas Cottrell first saw the dark figure going under the trolley bridge over Matawan Creek. He recognized the immediate danger and tried to warn the people of Matawan what was coming their way. In a sense, he became the Paul Revere of the drama. He resisted ridicule and kept spreading the warning that a large shark was in Matawan Creek. He was determined to accomplishment his mission. This was a matter of life and death.

When he approached the scene at the New Jersey Clay Company brickyard wharf, Joseph Dunn was in mortal danger and he assisted the rescuers in getting the injured boy into his boat. He then turned the boat and headed at top speed to the Wyckoff dock and medical help. Without his bold, decisive actions Joseph Dunn could have perished like Lester and Stanley. Captain Cottrell was not the type of man who could look the other way.

Stanley's old childhood friend, Willie Shephard also filled a special role on that tragic day. Willie was on the dock when Stanley was pulled out of the water. He saw the horrible wound and the look of extreme emotional anguish when Stanley said, "Oh my God" as he saw his own torn and mutilated leg. Willie was there to try to calm Stanley down so Dr. Reynolds could treat him. He helped carry Stanley up the hill to the railroad station. When Dr. Reynolds asked for a volunteer to ride on the train to Long Branch with Stanley, Willie was there to be with his dear friend. As the train left Matawan Station,

Willie was on the floor of the aisle next to Stanley trying to keep him alert and conscious. During the ride to Long Branch, Willie may have thought back to that time in 1903 when he was the victim who had fallen off Stanley's shoulders and hit his head while they were fooling around. This was certainly a reversal of roles played by the two close friends.

Willie was with Stanley at the hospital until the end. It was a consolation to the grieving Fisher family to know that Stanley's last moments on earth were with his good friend Willie Shephard. He was certainly a man who could not look the other way when his dear friend needed him.

In the small Bayshore town of Matawan, New Jersey on July 12, 1916 there were many people who behaved admirably. The feeling of being a caring neighbor and good friend brought out the best qualities in seemingly average people. Could this mutual feeling of good will bring some sort of closure to this shaken and grieving community?

Chapter | **X**

Life Goes On

As time moved forward from the trauma and stress of the shark attack, there were some changes and adjustments for several of the remaining characters in this story. Captain and Mrs. Fisher were not quite as active as they once had been, and spent more time at their home on Fountain Avenue. Agusta Nichols and her family were firmly established in their home in Minnesota and it was unlikely that they would ever return to Matawan. Arthur Nichols was now in demand as a landscape architect and he was involved in many significant projects. Mrs. Fisher spent more time visiting in Minnesota. Captain Fisher occasionally accompanied her on these longer visits, but he also remained in Matawan often, to take care of the house.

In 1922 Mrs. Fisher passed away. Her last years had been filled with sadness. She was laid to rest at the Fisher plot near Stanley, her daughter Florence, and her Mother in Rose Hill Cemetery. It was difficult for Captain Fisher to visit the grave site with all the memories that reminded him of better times.

Captain Fisher, alone now in Matawan, lived a few more years but would experience some health issues at his advancing age. He tried to visit his family in Minnesota but it was becoming more difficult for him to travel. Finally, in 1928 he died of pneumonia while on a visit to his daughter in Minneapolis. His funeral was at his beloved home on Fountain Avenue in Matawan. There were many people who attended the funeral. Everyone in town knew Captain Fisher and his family. He was greatly respected for his distinguished career. At this sad time, his friends and neighbors also remembered Stanley. Stanley's experience of the shark attack was briefly mentioned in Captain Fisher's obituary in the *Matawan Journal*. It was so unfortunate that Stanley had died just when Captain Fisher was beginning his retirement years.

Agusta Fisher Nichols, still living in Minnesota did her best to keep Stanley's memory alive through the coming years. She sent flowers on a regular basis to the Methodist Church in Matawan to honor Stanley's memory. It was still very hard for her to let Stanley go. In her poem that she wrote for the dedication for the Fisher window in 1918, she lamented that the family never had a chance to say good-bye to Stanley. Agusta was now the last remaining member of this very close family. She told stories to her children, especially her daughter Peggy, about her Uncle Stanley and his bravery at Matawan Creek. After all,

Agusta had been pregnant with Peggy at the time of the shark attack in 1916. Peggy visited her Uncle Stanley's grave at Rose Hill Cemetery in the early 1920s.

The Stillwell family continued to live in Matawan. Lester's older brothers and sisters matured as adults and remained in the area. Lester's oldest brother, Harry, served as a sergeant in the army during World War II. Lester's father, William Stillwell, passed away in 1944, and his Mother Luella died in 1946. His older brothers survived into the 1950s. They all had fond memories and sorrows about their young brother, Lester, who had such a short tragic life.

Albert O'Hara, Lester's young friend down at the Wyckoff dock, had some difficulties in the years following the shark attack. In 1919, at the age of 14, he was arrested by the police for stealing $20 in cash from the register of a local butcher's shop. He was sent to juvenile court in Freehold, New Jersey, the county seat of Monmouth County. Later in the 1920s he was arrested twice for transporting illegal liquor during Prohibition. One of his offences was for resisting arrest by threatening the policeman who stopped him. It seemed that he had difficulty conforming to the normal behavior expected by society.

Frank Clowes, the oldest boy at the Wyckoff dock, and Willie Shephard, Stanley Fisher's close friend, enlisted in the navy during World War I. They returned home to Matawan after the war as veterans and joined the local American Legion Post 176. Willie Shephard eventually became "Commander" of the Post. He also worked for the prosecutor's office in Freehold and then became tax collector in Matawan. He was highly respected and active in town affairs. He died in 1950 of a heart attack. He was buried in Rose Hill Cemetery about 20 yards from his lifelong fried Stanley Fisher.

George "Red" Burlew, who dove down in Matawan Creek with Stanley Fisher searching for Lester's body, became an active fisherman in Keyport after the incident. His father, Edward Burlew, had been a commercial fisherman for years. In 1934 Red Burlew and his wife Elizabeth moved to Brielle, New Jersey, along the Jersey shore. He became involved in sport fishing and was a guide and captain of a charter vessel. He was very successful in this activity and eventually moved to the east coast of Florida, where he gained a reputation as an outstanding big-game fishing guide. His efforts led to many record breaking catches in tuna and sharks. For years he vividly remembered the 1916 shark attack and the tragic end of his good friend Stanley Fisher. Red lived a long life and died in the 1980s.

Arthur Smith, the other man diving in the water with Stanley Fisher and Red Burlew, continued his life as a carpenter in Matawan. He later became blind but lived into his 90s. At the Wyckoff dock the shark had brushed by him, before it attacked Stanley. When asked about the shark attack, he would lift his shirt and show the marks on his body. He was 51 years old in 1916, but he certainly did his part as if he were a much younger man.

Johnson Cartan, one of the boys at the Wyckoff dock, stayed in Matawan for the rest of his life. He became a popular attorney in town. He would tell the story of the powerful churning in the water just before the shark attacked Lester. He saw the shark on the surface, when it lifted Lester several times out of the water. He said the shark first looked like a partially submerged log. He was frustrated along with the other boys when the people in town did not believe them when they first tried to report what had just happened at the Wyckoff dock. However, Stanley Fisher understood that there was real trouble and rushed down to the scene of the attack to try to help Lester.

Jacob Lefferts, the local Matawan attorney who jumped into the water at the New Jersey Clay Company brickyard wharf, to help Joseph Dunn, was 35 years old in 1916. He became a land developer in Matawan and was instrumental in creating two man-made lakes in town. In 1924 Lake Matawan was created when a dam was constructed to block Gravelly Creek. A second lake, Lake Lefferts was created when a dam was built on Matawan Creek in 1929. At this time "the Crick" was no longer used for commercial purposes. The New York-Long Branch Railroad provided a better alternative for heavy load cargo transportation to New York. The new dam lowered the depth of Matawan Creek but it still meandered out to Raritan Bay.

Koert Wyckoff, Stanley's friend, and Meta Thompson Wyckoff, Stanley's former girlfriend, spent the rest of their married life in Matawan. Koert became the tax collector in town and Meta enjoyed her musical activities. She was the Methodist Church organist at times. Koert died in 1966 and Meta died in 1976. It is interesting to note that Koert died 50 years after Stanley's death in 1916 and Meta died 60 years after Stanley's death. The three of them always maintained friendly personal relations. Koert sang a solo at Lester Stillwell's burial service, and he was a pall bearer at Stanley's funeral later that same day. Koert and Stanley sang together in the Quintet in happier times. Now Stanley, Lester, Koert, Meta, Captain Cottrell, and Willie Shephard are all together again in Rose Hill Cemetery.

Joseph Dunn, the only survivor of the 1916 shark attacks, left Saint Peter's Hospital in New Brunswick in September of 1916. The doctors were able to save his leg, even with the significant injuries. He had received treatment rather quickly and fortunately the artery was not severed. Joseph had enjoyed talking to the reporters from the different newspapers at the time, but he wanted to get out of the hospital and try to resume his young life again. Joseph's father, was overwhelmed with all of the letters, telegrams, and publicity. It was important for the family to resume their former life back in New York City.

The Hourihan family had lived in Matawan for generations. Jerry Hourihan, Senior who helped Michael Dunn rescue Joseph from the shark did not discuss the 1916 incident with his family for many years. His son Jerry Hourihan, Jr. said his father relayed the story to him in 1953 when a construction project was being done near Matawan Creek. Jerry Hourihan, Sr., said that most people in Matawan remembered the shark attack at the Wyckoff dock but the attack on the Cliffwood side of the creek, near the New Jersey Clay Company brickyard wharf was mostly forgotten because it did not actually happen in Matawan. This attack was lower on Matawan Creek, between Matawan and Keyport Harbor. People in recent years realize that this event was really the second chapter of this evolving tragedy, that impacted many lives at the time.

As time passed, the people of Matawan lived through the roaring twenties, Prohibition, the Great Depression, World War II, the Cold War, and now the problems of the 21st century.

However, the older residents in town sometimes stopped for a moment to reflect when they passed the Fisher house on Fountain Avenue, the Stillwell House on Church Street, the original Matawan railroad station, which still stands unused, and when they walked along the banks of the "Crick." It seems that some memories become part of a town, even as time moves forward.

Chapter

Matawan Creek Touches Other Lives

In compiling research for my historical talks about Matawan, I have literally read through thousands of pages of the old *Matawan Journal* from the 1870s to the 1970s when it stopped publication. The paper typically had 8 pages to an issue with very small print. The *Journal* was very thorough about covering local events. Everyone in the town and surrounding area subscribed to it. I became absorbed in this task and would sit for hours turning the delicate pages of the original issues.

I noticed that the people of the town had a strong, emotional tie to the "Crick" before and after the shark attacks in 1916. To many growing up in town, this meandering waterway was a special mystical place. It was part of a Matawan childhood.

Matawan was not a particularly safe place in the early part of the 20th Century. Aside from the famous shark attacks, there were many accidents along the streets and railroad lines, fires, and other tragedies that impacted small town life. In fact, three people in one family were killed along the railroad tracks at different times. From the fall of 1918 to the spring of 1919 sixty-five people died from the devastating pandemic of the Spanish Influenza. Early death was not unusual in Matawan.

Every summer, people died in boating accidents and surf type drownings with under tow along the Jersey shore. The waves would get too high and swamp a boat, killing several on board. The ocean could also be deadly and unpredictable with changes in weather.

To many young people, Matawan Creek seemed a better, safer place to take a swim. The "Crick" was more predictable and located in the center of town, where neighbors and workers were nearby if something happened. However, there were two incidents in particular, that resembled the drama of the 1916 shark attacks, involving young people and courageous efforts on the part of others. One incident happened about three weeks before the 1916 shark attack and the other eight years later, almost to the exact anniversary of the 1916 attack.

On June 19, 1916, Raymond Thompson, age 11, and Frederick Thompson, age 7, were playing down at the old Wyckoff dock. Raymond knew how to swim and his mother had given him permission to take a dip in the creek. His younger brother, Frederick, wanted to splash around in the water but he was denied permission because he was unable to swim. He did take off his shoes and stockings and dangled his feet off the side of the dock. As Raymond enjoyed himself jumping off the old pilings, Frederick was watching his brother and became distracted. He fell off the dock and was drawn into a deep part of the creek. He felt himself going under and screamed to his brother for help. Raymond quickly moved in that direction, and saved his brother's life, just as Frederick was about to go underwater again. The *Matawan Journal* praised the young rescuer and the town breathed a sigh of relief. It was fortunate that Raymond quickly saw what was happening and could react immediately. Any delay could have cost Frederick his life. Many people in town exclaimed, "God watches over young children." All of the churches in Matawan said a prayer of thanks the following Sunday. No one at this time could anticipate the tragedy that would happen three weeks later to Stanley and Lester at the same Wyckoff dock.

Eight years later, on July 13, 1924, two brothers, Edward Hubbard, age 17, and Albert Hubbard, age 15, were "crabbing" under the drawbridge on the lower part of Matawan Creek between Matawan and Keyport. The boys had been doing this for years and were not nervous about this type of summer activity. They were standing on the side of the concrete abutment just under the bridge. Albert, the younger brother, who did not know how to swim, fell into Matawan Creek just below the bridge. Edward, who was a capable swimmer, jumped into the water to rescue his younger brother. In his failed effort to save his struggling brother who was in a panic state, both boys drown.

A crowd soon gathered at this location on Matawan Creek. Several men volunteered to try to recover the bodies of the two boys. Four men went out in a boat with long poles to prod the bottom of the creek to locate the bodies. However, the tide was coming in and this was causing difficulty. One man, Jack Haley, decided to dive to the bottom to see if he could find the bodies of Edward and Albert. With the tide coming in increasing the strength of the current under the bridge, the men submerged a long pole so that Haley could hold on to the pole while he pushed down to the bottom of the creek. By using this method, he was able to recover the body of the younger brother, Albert. When they brought Albert out of the water they tried to resuscitate him but failed.

The men continued to search for the body of the older brother, Edward, but the conditions were now becoming dangerous. They were finally able to locate Edward's body which was about eighteen feet away. The man who accomplished this was W. Scott Hopkins, a local fisherman. He was able to lift the body out of the water using oyster thongs. This sad days' work was finally over.

The town of Matawan was shocked again by this double death, which occurred almost exactly to the day, eight years after the 1916 shark attack. It seemed unusual that two brothers were involved again. But unlike the incident with the Dunn brothers where both of the brothers would survive the ordeal, the Hubbard brothers both perished.

It is interesting to note that Jack Haley, a brave volunteer, dove to the bottom of Matawan Creek to recover Alfred Hubbard's body, just like Stanley Fisher dove to the bottom of Matawan Creek to try to recover Lester Stillwell's body. Jack Haley was viewed as a hero, just like Stanley Fisher. Haley was a shy, modest man, who did not seek or want publicity. Haley had also been recognized as a hero a few years before, when he rescued a boy who had fallen through the ice in a pond while ice skating near the Matawan railroad station.

The Hubbard tragedy had another sad aspect associated with it. The family was very poor and Mr. Hubbard was unable to work due to an industrial accident. In fact, Edward Hubbard had gone to work in a brickyard to help support the family. Albert Hubbard was still in Matawan High School. The family did not have enough money to pay for the funeral and burials of their two sons. The local klavern of the Ku Klux Klan donated $50 to help with the expenses. In the 1920s the Klan had several thousand members in Monmouth County and five million throughout the United States. The Hubbard's really needed the money. Several local fraternal lodges made donations also. The Hubbard brothers were buried in Rose Hill Cemetery on the other side of the hill from Stanley Fisher.

The Hubbard family put a memorial poem to their dead sons in the *Matawan Journal*:

Short and sudden was the call

Of our dear sons who were loved by all

The blow was great, the shock severe

We little thought their deaths so near

Only those who have lost can tell

The pain of departing without farewell

Mr. and Mrs. Hubbard, sister and brother

This poem was very similar to the poem that Agusta Fisher Nichols wrote about her brother Stanley Fisher in that both families lamented the fact that their loved ones had been taken from them suddenly, and that they did not have a chance to say, "Good-bye."

No one swims in Matawan Creek in the 21st Century. When the dam was built to create Lake Lefferts in 1929 the depth of the creek was dramatically reduced. In recent years I have taken many history buffs, researchers, newspaper reporters, radio hosts and film people down to the location of the old Wyckoff dock. The dock no longer exists in any form. Even in 1916 it was abandoned and in a dilapidated condition. People are surprised when they see Matawan Creek now. It is shallow and overgrown with vegetation. It is still narrow and meanders through Matawan "like a snake," but when I close my eyes and let my imagination go, I can still hear the kids laughing and splashing around in the muddy waters of the "crick."

Chapter

Stanley's Descendants Remember

Stanley Fisher was a young man in the prime of life, when he met his untimely, tragic death. He was a popular, outgoing man who had not yet married. He was very close to his immediate family, and especially to his older sister, Agusta. In fact, when Stanley was treated at the Wyckoff dock by Dr. Reynolds, Stanley said to his close friend, Willie Shephard, to care for his sister if he would not survive the ordeal. Willie nodded in agreement as he tried to calm and reassure his friend.

When the family returned to Matawan after Stanley's death Agusta was pregnant with her second child. After the funeral ceremonies she and her family stayed with her parents for a while before returning to Minneapolis. Her new daughter Adella Louise Nichols, called "Peggy", was born on January 5, 1917.

Through the years Agusta had been extremely close to her younger brother Stanley and she was proud of the man he had grown up to be. She had lost a younger sister, Florence, to pneumonia at an earlier time before Stanley was born. Stanley was a special gift to the grieving family after that sad time. Now, another period of sadness set in on the Fisher family to endure. Agusta's children, especially Peggy, would grow up hearing about the merits of her Uncle Stanley and about his heroic sacrifice at Matawan Creek. Until her death in the 1967, Agusta would send flowers regularly.

Although Agusta's daughter Peggy never met her Uncle Stanley, she had visited his grave as a little girl and felt real admiration for this special man. She grew up in Minnesota and attended Cornell College in Mount Vernon, Iowa and then received a B.A. Degree from the University of Minnesota in 1940. She became a renowned pianist, and studied under Dimetri Metropoulos, the conductor of the Minneapolis Symphony Orchestra. During World War II she was a "grey lady" with the Red Cross at the Veteran's Hospital in Minneapolis. She married Dr. Howard Andersen in 1942.

After the war, they moved to Rochester, Minnesota, where Dr. Andersen joined the staff of the Mayo Clinic. Peggy became involved in local community activities sharing her exceptional musical talent. Peggy was always aware of the special place that her Uncle Stanley had in history. She received the Rose Hill Cemetery newsletter annually and often sent flowers to be placed on Stanley's grave to honor his memory. Peggy had two sons and a daughter. Both sons eventually became medical doctors like their father Dr. Howard Andersen. The children also heard stories about their special relative and had a real desire to preserve his memory. They saw pictures of Stanley Fisher and would learn more about him as the shark attack books and films appeared in later years.

I had the special privilege to speak to Peggy Andersen in 2012 after Hurricane Sandy devastated the Jersey shore area. Peggy called the Matawan Historical Society to see if anyone knew if the hurricane had damaged the Fisher grave site area in Rose Hill Cemetery. I responded to her call in my role as the Matawan Town Historian and vice-president of the Rose Hill Cemetery Company. I assured her that I had recently visited the grave site and that all was well, with no damage to the stones.

Peggy and I had a pleasant conversation about her Uncle Stanley. I shared with her the fact that I conducted historical tours of Rose Hill Cemetery, and made a special effort to discuss the 1916 shark attack and Stanley Fisher's heroic sacrifice to try to recover the body of Lester Stillwell. She was pleased to hear that many visitors to the cemetery commented on Stanley's heroism and felt inspired by his actions. I was amazed at the amount of information her mother, Agusta, had passed on to her about her Uncle Stanley. I was able to tell her a few details about her mother, father, and Uncle Stanley that she had not heard before. In closing she said that she would like to come to Matawan and visit Stanley's grave and the graves of her grand-parents. However, she reminded me that she was 95 years old and she did not get around much. We agreed to keep in touch.

I was very sad when I received a letter from Dr. Richard Andersen telling me that his mother, Peggy, had died on December 1, 2013 at the age of 96. He provided me with a copy of her obituary and said that he would like to keep in touch. He asked that the Rose Hill Cemetery newsletter be sent to his home address. I told him we would be happy to comply and that I would personally continue to honor Stanley Fisher's memory through the cemetery tours and my historical lectures on the 1916 shark attack. I was very pleased that the Andersen family tradition was going to continue in the next generation.

As we approach the 100th anniversary of the shark attack in 2016, the story continues to inspire many people who are looking for heroes and role models in a world that is unpredictable and changing at a rapid pace. I feel very encouraged when children and young adults approach me on the cemetery tours and want to know more about that brave young man, Stanley Fisher. I have been searching for details for decades about this man and I truly believe that his story is worth remembering. I also feel good when I see that visitors to the cemetery often leave little mementos behind to remind Lester and Stanley that their grave sites have been visited. Lester's gifts include baseball gloves, stuffed animals, and other toys. Stanley's gifts are representative of courage like American flags, medals for heroism, and other symbols of manhood. I am sure that Stanley and Lester are smiling when they watch these admiring visitors paying them genuine respect. If Stanley could respond, I think he would say," I just did my duty."

Chapter

Stanley's Values Today?

If Stanley Fisher could return to his old hometown today and talk to residents, listen to talk radio, watch television, and use the internet, what would he think of the world one hundred years after his death? Would he be pleased? Would he understand the changes that have taken place? Would he see many of his values still in effect? In every generation since humans started living on this planet, there have been good people, and selfish, evil people. If we look at facts and avoid personal observations and opinions, we may be able to see what has happened over the last one hundred years since that tragic day in Matawan on July 12, 1916. Stanley will have to look at the big picture and make up his own mind.

In Stanley's world of 1916, men dominated most activities in politics and on the domestic scene. Women did not acquire the vote until 1920. There were many influential women, including Queen Victoria and other notable individuals like Helen Keller and popular female authors. However, most women were seen as responsible for maintaining the household and raising children. Men were expected to have a career or a meaningful job to provide for the family. The concept of manhood had a real psychological and practical place in society. It seems that Stanley was trying to fulfill this traditional view of manhood in his outlook on life.

There were significant changes in the role of women during World War I and even more during the World War II years. Then women actually took over male jobs to keep the country going and the war effort strong. Today women have achieved an equal role in most facets of modern society. If you use the term "manhood" in a serious way, you could be criticized for being "anti-women", which would be totally inappropriate.

However, this ideal of growing into an adult role in society has not really changed. Now, girls want to achieve womanhood just like serious boys want to grow up to be men. Everyone now recognizes that women, like men, are presidents of countries (not just queens), CEOs of great multi-national corporations, leaders in research and science, in the media and the military and every other meaningful activity. Confident males do not resent this development. They relish the competition, and it is real competition.

In Stanley's time, his mother, grandmother, and sister fulfilled the traditional roles for women. But if Stanley had lived longer, he would have seen his niece, Peggy Nichols Andersen, born in 1917, become a well-respected leader in cultural activities in Rochester, Minnesota. She was a concert pianist who performed with the Minneapolis Symphony Orchestra. Yes, I think Stanley would see women in this new role. He was a fair minded person who showed respect to everyone.

Stanley certainly believed that courage under fire and a sense of duty were important values to strive for in life. Today there are people who are always looking out for themselves, and consider self- interest above the welfare of others at all times. However, there are also people like Stanley, both men and women, who have dedicated their lives, even risking and sacrificing their lives, to save the lives of others who they do not even know in a personal sense. We see many examples every day of military personnel and first responders, police, and fire fighters, who run toward the danger instead of away.

In Stanley's time devotion to ones' immediate family was of paramount value and often taken for granted in everyday life. This is an area today that Stanley might find troubling and hard to understand from his perspective. As you study sociology you see that the traditional family has undergone significant changes since 1916. A number of marriages now end in divorce. Children are sometimes put in the horrible situation of deciding which parent to live with through court proceedings. Joint custody can also be a very confusing and frustrating for a child.

Today, many immediate family members do not live in the same area due to employment requirements. To many people having a happy family life is a goal rather than a reality. There are also many single parent homes and non-traditional relationships. Everyone wants a happy home to go to, but the traditional family unit is not always an option. Sometimes, grandparents take over the leading role in a family unit.

Stanley always counted on his immediate family for support. He lived at home at 4 Fountain Avenue until his death. I saw the Matawan voting records for November, 1915, where Stanley signed his name next to his father, Captain Watson Fisher, both living at the family home. When Stanley went to Minnesota from 1911-February of 1915 to learn the dry cleaning trade, he lived with his sister, Agusta, and her family. Stanley would probably find this family living apart trend in society hard to understand and accept.

Even though Stanley came from a prominent, financially secure family in town, he was never a "snob." He always viewed everyone, rich or poor, with the same respect. In his work in the YMCA he enjoyed helping kids improve their physical skills, so they could enjoy group athletics. He had a special concern for Lester Stillwell, a poor boy who experienced epileptic seizures. He had probably seen this and worried about Lester on the day of the shark attack, with all of the confusion, when the boys ran through town naked shouting that Lester was gone. He was concerned that something had definitely happened to Lester.

There are many people today who are very concerned about those who are less fortunate than they are in society. America is a very generous country. There are wealthy benefactors and every day middle class citizens who make financial sacrifices to help the sick and the poor, even in other countries, when there is a natural disaster.

Stanley would be pleased to see that helping those who are less fortunate is still of value that is important to many Americans, and that class consciousness does not get in the way of doing the right thing for people who need help.

Stanley Fisher was a member of an organized church in Matawan, the Methodist Episcopal Church, which was located in the center of town. He was a soloist in the choir and leader of the Sunday School. Religion was very much a part of his life. When he sang in the Quintet group one of his favorite songs was the emotionally moving "Onward Christian Soldiers." The Quintet often sang this hymn at events other than church related venues. If Stanley would sing this hymn at the town square today, how would it be received by the public? Would people smile and sing along with him? Would they laugh at him? In 1916, religious faith was a real support for families that faced many personal tragedies. It was so important to believe in God who would help you face the challenges and uncertainties of life.

Today organized religion has experienced many obstacles including a decrease in active membership and numerous court cases involving religious issues. Most Americans claim to believe in a God, or superior being, but they do not always believe it is necessary to belong to an organized church. They consider themselves spiritual or religious in their own way. It is not necessary to sit in church on a Sunday morning to be a good person. In fact, some church goers are viewed as hypocrites who do not follow through with their beliefs the rest of the week.

On the other hand, there are many people who still find comfort in going to church and raising their children with a formal religious faith. Stanley would hear the church bells ring and watch the children going to Sunday school and follow them into the church. He would probably be looking for his choir robe as he was preparing to participate in the service.

Stanley in the last moments of this life held true to his values. He wanted the attending surgeon to know that he did his duty. Today there are many examples of people who have recognized the fact that they were dying and held true to the values that had always supported them. On the morning of September 11, 2001, passengers on the doomed flights called home to their loved ones to say for one last time, "I love you." In some cases, this final message was said to an answering machine. Firefighters were rushing up the staircases while others were streaming down to safety. Men and women were holding hands as they jumped to their deaths with the flames behind them. There are many stories of heroism that will never be told. Even in the twenty-first century there are people like Stanley who go to their untimely deaths with courage and dignity.

After weighing all the conflicting data, I think Stanley would conclude that times have changed and there is still hope for humanity, but it is important to have strong values and know that you are moving in the right direction when the world seems to be falling apart around you.

Chapter

Public Interest Revives in Shark Attacks

Today, one hundred years later, if you travel around the United States, as well as parts of the world, and you mention the 1916 New Jersey shark attacks, there are people who recognize this event and are eager to talk about it. They have seen documentaries, movies, or read books about the people involved in this tragedy. How did this special interest in a distant historical incident come about?

In the several decades following the 1916 shark attacks most people in Matawan, quite naturally, went about their daily lives. Events of the time became primary. If you were not directly related to someone involved in the shark attacks, the memories had a tendency to fade away. There were two notable exceptions to this. If you were a person involved in the study of marine science and shark behavior, or if you were an avid history buff, the 1916 shark attacks still had a special interest for you. It was a unique situation that did not fit the normal pattern of experience.

In 1974, Peter Benchley released his novel, *JAWS*. A year later in 1975, the blockbuster movie, *JAWS* was released by Universal Pictures. It is considered one of the greatest films ever made, and was the highest grossing film of all time until the release of *STAR WARS* in 1977. Starring in the movie were Roy Scheider, Richard Dreyfuss and Robert Shaw. The movie introduced a serial killer great white shark that terrorized a seaside town during the summer holiday season. In addition to providing thrilling entertainment the movie generated a fear of shark attacks as Americans enjoyed their summer fun at the beach. Richard Dreyfuss, playing a marine scientist, refers to the brutal New Jersey shark attacks of 1916. This reference to an historical incident fostered curiosity among the public about shark attacks in the past.

In July 1916 there were several shark attacks during a twelve-day period along the Jersey Shore. The first attack happened on July 1 at Beach Haven, New Jersey. A young business man, Charles Vansant, from Philadelphia was attacked by a shark while swimming at the beach in front of the Engleside Hotel. He had severe wounds to his upper leg and died a short time after he was brought from the beach. If there had been a way to provide immediate hospital care, he may have survived. Sadly, there were no medivac helicopters to transport him in those days.

The second shark attack happened at Spring Lake, New Jersey, forty-three miles north of Beach Haven on July 6, 1916. Charles Bruder, the bell captain at the Essex and Sussex Hotel, was attacked by a shark during his afternoon swim, and died immediately because his two lower legs were bitten off by the shark. He bled to death before any medical assistance could be provided.

On July 12, in Matawan, the next shark attacks happened at the Wyckoff dock and the New Jersey Clay Company brickyard wharf along Matawan Creek. Lester Stillwell and Stanley Fisher died on the same day, but Joseph Dunn survived the attack after being hospitalized for several months. There is also a dilemma among scholars of whether the killer shark was a juvenile great white or a bull shark. Both sharks are man eaters, but the bull shark has the unique ability to move from salt water to fresh water. The final decision is still being debated by proponents from both sides of the issue.

Before 1916 many marine scientists did not think of sharks as particularly dangerous to humans, or that they swam as far north as they do. After these events, many people viewed the shark, rightly or wrongly, as a fierce predator ready to strike unsuspecting victims at the beach. This created a great fear of the unknown.

Television documentaries have also played a significant role in keeping the Jersey shark attacks of 1916 in front of the viewing audience. The annual "Shark Week" television programming has brought out the historical aspects of this observance with references to Lester Stillwell, Stanley Fisher, and the eccentric figure of Captain Cottrell. The motion picture industry since *JAWS* has also been interested in portraying the drama of the 1916 shark attacks. Movie companies from the United States, United Kingdom, Republic of South Africa and Canada have all produced films in recent years on this topic. The author was also a consultant to a Canadian film company working on a shark attack project in Matawan.

In 2006, on the ninetieth anniversary of the shark attack, the town of Matawan started an event called "Shark fest". This involved speeches and a wreath laying ceremony at the graves of Stanley Fisher and Lester Stilwell in the morning and street fair activities and displays in the downtown area in the afternoon. This event was reported very well in the local press and media, and the event was repeated for several more years.

In 2011 a "cemetery tour" of the local Rose Hill Cemetery was started by the Matawan Historical Society. This tour not only recognizes Lester Stillwell and Stanley Fisher, but also highlights others involved with the shark attacks, as well as people of local interest.

While taking another look at these events from the perspective of the Twenty first century, the person of Stanley Fisher became more intriguing. In so many ways Stanley represents the values and belief structure of that distant historical period. Stanley was willing to risk everything, his physical well-being, his future prospects, his very life, for a young friend, Lester, who sometimes had the shakes and needed special help. Stanley was not a reckless man. He was careful about so many things in his life, but at the critical moment when decisive action was required, he "did his duty". This is one of those times when real life tops a fictional script.

Many in the Twenty-first century are still amazed by this story. People will always be searching for the fortitude to face uncertain times. With the prospect of terrorism happening in local communities, people wonder "what would I do if faced by a life or death situation in my daily life?" Would I be able to do what is necessary to protect my family and friends? With this in mind, Stanley Fisher has become a role model for many concerned individuals around the world.

Chapter

EPILOGUE

My quest to identify and describe the "real Stanley Fisher" has been an obsession of mine for several decades. I first became familiar with Stanley Fisher's name when I moved to Matawan forty-five years ago. Being a history buff since my early days at historic Gettysburg College, I knew about the series of shark attacks along the Jersey Coast in 1916, but I did not learn the specific details about the Matawan Creek incident until I joined the Matawan Historical Society in the 1970s. I spoke to members who knew what happened from their parents and grandparents. I became fascinated with the story of this courageous young man Stanley Fisher who died in such unusual and tragic circumstances.

With my growing involvement with the Matawan Historical Society through the years, along with several historical projects, like my Rose Hill Cemetery tours, I wanted to learn more about Stanley Fisher as a person. The articles and monographs written about the shark attack did not deal with his background, early life, his feelings and his personality.

Stanley was only twenty-four years old, beginning his business career, when he met his tragic, untimely end. He did not leave behind a diary or personal letters for research purposes. I know he was deeply loved by his immediate family, who were heartbroken at the time of his death and not inclined to share many personal memories with others. They did make arrangements for the completion of the memorial stained glass window, the Bethlehem window, to be placed in the front of the Methodist Church, to honor their son. Stanley's sister, Agusta, wrote a beautiful poem which was published in the *Matawan Journal*. However, that is where the story ended with regard to Stanley's private life.

As I pursued my research through the years, I was able to learn about the personal side of Stanley Fisher in other ways. I spoke to people who knew the Fisher family and friends of their family. I gradually saw a character emerging who represented a different historical period, with special ideas and values.

A pleasant surprise was when I was able to speak to Peggy Nichols Andersen, Stanley's niece, who never actually met him, but learned about Stanley through the warm, loving stories her Mother told her about her Uncle Stanley. Her fondness for him lasted for her lifetime of ninety-six years.

I also had an advantage as a researcher, because the Fisher family was very prominent in Matawan. There were many items and news briefs written in the *Matawan Journal* about the family from the 1880s until the 1920s, ending with the deaths of Captain and Mrs. Fisher. I followed Stanley's progress through the years in school, his athletic accomplishments, his leadership role in many activities, his singing career, his social life, and his return to Matawan to begin his new dry cleaning and tailoring business.

Although Stanley did not speak to me directly by way of a diary or personal letters, I felt that I was gradually getting to know him through his actions and interactions with others, and how people close to him referred to their friend, Stanley Fisher. They used many adjectives to describe his character and personality such as noble, dependable, caring, fun loving, family-oriented, courageous, physically strong, a true leader, talented, protective of the weak, and religious. It seemed to me, over and over, that everyone in town, young and old, saw Stanley as a fine, genuine young man who really cared about others and had a great deal to contribute to Matawan. I can see how the town was really devastated with his tragic death.

After looking at him from different angles in my research over the years, I feel very confident to say that my early impressions of him were correct. He was an exceptional young man with admirable values which came out at the time of the mortal crisis of his young life. His nobility of spirit was evident until he took his very last breath.

In 2016 the town of Matawan will host different events to commemorate the 100th anniversary of the 1916 shark attack. Through the years this incident has become part of the historic folklore of New Jersey, like Washington crossing the Delaware, the crash of the German dirigible the Hindenburg, the wreck of the passenger ship Morro Castle, and the famous Lindbergh baby kidnapping and trial, that became a major national event. Books and movies about the shark attack distributed around the world have created significant public interest in what happened in a small New Jersey town in 1916.

As a historian, I truly believe we can learn from events of the past and how everyday people are able to respond to unbelievable challenges. Stanley Fisher certainly fulfills this role for readers. His story reflects the best elements of human nature and is still relevant as we move forward in the 21st Century.

APPENDIX A

Chronology of Fisher Family and Matawan Shark Attack Events

1879 - Captain and Mrs. Watson Fisher move to Matawan

1892 - Stanley is born in New York City and returns home to Matawan

1897 - Stanley enters Glenwood Institute

1907 - Agusta Fisher marries Arthur Nichols and moves
to Minnesota

1909 - Stanley graduates from Matawan High School
and enters Freehold Military Academy

1911 - Stanley leaves Freehold Military Academy and
goes to Minnesota to learn the dry cleaning trade

1915 - Stanley returns to Matawan and begins dry
cleaning business on Main Street

1916 - July 1, Charles Vansant is attacked by a shark in
Beach Haven and dies the same day

July 6, Charles Bruder is attacked by a shark in
Spring Lake and dies immediately

July 12, Lester Stillwell is attacked by a shark and
dies immediately

Stanley Fisher is attacked by the same shark;
dies later same day

Joseph Dunn is attacked by shark but survives
his wounds

July 14, Lester Stillwell's body surfaces in
Matawan Creek near train trestle

Michael Schleisser captures and kills a great
white shark on Raritan Bay

July 15, Lester Stillwell and Stanley Fisher funerals and burial at Rose Hill Cemetery

September 15, Joseph Dunn discharged from Saint Peter's Hospital in New Brunswick

1917 - January 5, Peggy Nichols, niece of Stanley Fisher, is born in Minnesota

1918 - Spring, Fisher Memorial window is installed in the First Methodist Episcopal Church

October 4-6, explosion at the Morgan Ammunition Loading Depot damages window

1922 - Mrs. Watson Fisher dies in Matawan

1924 - Edward and Albert Hubbard drown in Matawan Creek

1928 - Captain Watson Fisher dies while visiting daughter in Minnesota

1967 - June 24, Agusta Fisher Nichols, Stanley's sister, dies in Minnesota

1970 - First Methodist Episcopal Church torn down; Fisher window auctioned off

1974 - The novel *JAWS* by Peter Benchley appears and is very successful

1975 - The blockbuster movie *JAWS* is released

2001 - Dr. Richard Fernicola's book, *Twelve Days of Terror* is released

Michael Capuzzo's book, *Close to Shore* is released

2006 - Matawan Shark fest begins, in commemoration of the ninetieth anniversary

2009 - British film, *Blood in the Water* is released

2013 - December 7, Peggy Nichols Anderson, Stanley's niece, dies at age 96 in Minnesota

2016 - July 9 to July 17, Matawan conducts nine-day
commemoration of one hundredth anniversary

July 17, dedication of memorial monument to
Lester Stillwell and Stanley Fisher

APPENDIX B

Pictures of Historic Matawan

Main Street Matawan, Trolley Line and Horse Hitching Post

Early Vehicle Transportation

Matawan Creek Winding Through Town

Early Post Office

Matawan's First Library

Matawan Bank on Main Street

Flaked Rice Factory near Railroad Station

Matawan Tile Company

Summer Mud on Main Street

Main Street in Winter

Glenwood Institute

First Matawan High School

Odd Fellows Social Hall

First Methodist Episcopal Church, Main Street

Matawan Commercial Block

Smaller Stores on Lower Main Street

Trolley Bridge Over Matawan Creek

Site of Wyckoff Dock on Matawan Creek

Main Street Looking in Direction of Wyckoff Dock

Photograph of Lester Stillwell (New Brunswick Times)

Portrait Photograph of Stanley Fisher

Matawan Railroad Station

Matawan House Hotel, Main Street

Matawan Creek Near Ravine Drive

Early Matawan Fireman

Farmers and Merchants Bank, Main Street

*Matawan Water Works and Levet Manufacturing
Building on the Hill*

Burrowes Mansion, Site of Revolutionary War Raid, later home of Benjamin F.S. Brown, publisher of the Matawan Journal in 1916

First Baptist Church, Main Street

First Presbyterian Church, Main Street

Trinity Episcopal Church, Main Street

Main Street Looking Toward Matawan House Hotel

Rose Hill Cemetery, Central Mount

Rose Hill Cemetery, Lower Level

Matawan's First Fire Engine, 1869

Matawan's First Hook and Ladder Truck, 1877

Middletown Point Academy, First Preparatory School, 1830

Matawan's First Separate Building Post Office, 1930's

Shark Hunting Boat in Matawan Creek
from New York World newspaper

Bibliography

Andersen, Mrs. "Peggy." (Niece of Stanley Fisher) Telephone conversation, Rochester, Minnesota, 2012.

Andersen, Dr. Richard D. (Grand-nephew of Stanley Fisher) Personal letter and obituary information, Aden Hills, Minnesota, 2014.

Asbury Park Press. (Various Issues) Asbury Park, New Jersey.

Benchley, Peter. *Jaws.* New York: Doubleday and Company, Inc., 1974.

Capuzzo, Michael. *Close to Shore.* New York: Broadway Books, 2001.

Ellis, Edward Robb. *Echoes of Distant Thunder: Life in the United States, 1914-1918.* New York: Coward McCann, and Geoghegan, Inc., 1975.

Ellis, Richard. *Book of Sharks.* New York: Grossett and Dunlop, 1975.

Fernicola, Dr. Richard G. *Twelve Days of Terror.* Guilford, CT: The Lyons Press, 2001.

Henderson, Elizabeth. (Lifelong resident of Matawan) Conversations, Matawan, NJ, 1976-2010.

Henderson, Helen. *Around Matawan and Aberdeen*. Dover, New Hampshire: Arcadia Publishing, 1996.

_____ *Matawan and Aberdeen: Of Town and Field*. Dover, NH: Arcadia Publishing, 2003.

_____*From Backstreet to Main Street...and Beyond*. Keyport, NJ: Self Published, 2015.

Hourihan, Jerry, Jr. Conversations, Matawan, NJ 2008-2015.

Jones, Walter. (Former historian of First Methodist Episcopal Church of Matawan) Conversations, Matawan, NJ 2008-2015.

Keyport Weekly. Various Issues. Keyport, NJ.

Kisenwether, Rev. Louis W. *First Baptist Church in Matawan: A Constant Testimony*. Matawan, NJ: First Baptist Church, 2000.

Mandeville, Carol. (Grand-daughter of Koert and Meta Wyckoff) Conversations, Matawan, NJ, 2015.

Map of Matawan, NJ (1873). Matawan Historical Society Archives.

Map of Matawan, NJ (1889). Matawan Historical Society Archives.

Matawan Borough, NJ. (Voting Records 1915-1918).

Matawan Historical Society. (Archives and Historical Photographs). Matawan, NJ.

Matawan Journal. Issues 1879-1928, Matawan, NJ.

Matawan Journal: *100ᵗʰ* Anniversary Issue: Matawan, NJ: Brown Publishing and Printing Co., July 31, 1936.

Matawan-Aberdeen Public Library. Historical Documents. Matawan, NJ.

McKeen, Patricia. (Lifelong resident of Matawan and distant relation of Meta Thompson Wyckoff) Conversations, Matawan, NJ. 2010-2012.

Murphy, Audie. *To Hell and Back*. New York: Holt, Henry and Co. Inc., 2002.

New York Times. Various Issues. New York, NY.

Nichols, Arthur. (Brother-in-law of Stanley Fisher) Provided portrait photograph of Stanley Fisher to the Matawan Historical Society, 1966.

_____Provided Funeral Memorial Card of his wife, Agusta, Fisher Nichols, to the Matawan Historical Society, 1967.

Rose Hill Cemetery Company. (Map and Burial Records) Provided by J.A. Savolaine, Vice-President and Historian.

Savolaine, John A. *Hundred-Year-Old Structures of Matawan*. Matawan, NJ: Historic Sites Commission, 2015.

Skinner, Jennifer. Direct descendant of Captain Thomas Cottrell. Interview in Matawan March 20, 2016.

Smithsonian World War I: From Sarajevo to Versailles. New York: D.K. Publishing, 2014.

Wardell, Charles H. (Long-time resident hand written diaries 1856-1918) Matawan Historical Society, Matawan, NJ.

Woman's Club of Matawan. Historical Records 1915-1918.

About the Author

Al Savolaine received a B.A. degree from Gettysburg College, and a M.A. from Georgetown University. He served as a Captain in the U.S. Army Reserve during the Vietnam Era. He was a teacher and division headmaster at two prominent private schools in New Jersey. He is now retired, and is the Matawan Town Historian and the Historian of Rose Hill Cemetery. His historic cemetery tours have been very popular for many years. Al has written articles on local history and has appeared on radio and local television talk shows. He lives in Matawan with his wife, Cathy.